Obstacles

BOOK 1 of a series

By Princess Dionna

Obstacle

/ˈäbstək(ə)l/

noun

A thing that blocks one's way, prevents, or hinders

progress.

Love

/ləv/

noun

An intense feeling of deep affection.

When love and progress collide, only one can lead the way.

Prologue

The blue sky, once clear, was slowly overtaken by brooding gray clouds. Still, streaks of sunlight fought through, cutting through the storm like grace through grief—defiant, determined. Much like their love.

No matter the storms they had weathered—the obstacles, the soul-binding connection, the intensity of their pasts—what they had was undeniable. A union not easily shaken. Their love had only strengthened, magnified, illuminated… then multiplied. It was invincible.

They gave to each other like champions in a flawless rally—love exchanged back and forth with precision and passion, each action returned with more meaning than the last. All while chaos, hatred, and jealousy tried to break them from the outside. But none of that mattered. What mattered was *his* love for *her*, and *her* love for *him*.

He understood now—this was part of God's divine plan for his life. He thought about the years they may have crossed paths without knowing: in line at Popeye's, brushing shoulders at a nearby store. Maybe he had held the door for her once. Maybe she was the kind woman with guarded eyes—the kind love had not been kind to before.

These thoughts kept him company as he moved down the highway, headed toward the only woman who had ever held his soul.

His eyes stayed focused on the road, but his heart… his heart was already with her. Jagged Edge blared from his car speakers—90's R&B always managed to echo what he felt. He couldn't wait to touch her, to hold her. His heartbeat pounded like it was keeping time for something sacred. Every part of him was ready.

He was finally free—free of the last restraint.

Traffic crawled, thick and impatient. But his goal was simple—make it to her job before she clocked out. The time on his tan dashboard read 4:09 p.m. She got off at 4:30. He wanted to get there before 4:15, just in time to surprise her.

She loved surprises.

He took the Williams Drive exit. Trees flanked the street in full bloom, cradling the professional building at 3040 like a portrait frame. He pulled into the underground parking garage, and the music echoed off the concrete, painting the air with nostalgia. He parked beside her white car—*Winter*, she called it.

Leaving his driver's door open, he stepped out of his midnight-blue Infiniti and approached her car with purpose. He placed a bouquet of reddish-pink roses, tied with a single black satin ribbon, on the hood. Red and black—*their* colors, the signature of every moment that felt like them. He slipped a red velvet card into a glossy black envelope; her name printed in elegant silver foil. Inside were instructions. Her next destination. A place he had planned down to the finest detail.

4:25 p.m.

Soon, she'd be walking down those stairs, approaching the car that was now part of something bigger—a romantic gesture threaded with mystery. He wanted her to feel it: the thought, the care, the love. That she was the most amazing woman in his world.

Sliding back into his seat, the tan leather welcomed him like an old friend. The music was still playing as he pulled out of the garage, the bassline of his heart racing in rhythm. The plan was in motion.

Chapter 1

It had been seven hours since she'd heard from Beckett.

Most Fridays, she'd call him on her lunch break or after her morning meeting—just to hear his voice. But today wasn't like most Fridays. Today was the day the court finalized the papers. No more legal tangles. No more custody hearings. Today was the beginning of something new—for both of them.

And still… silence.

Fear had been sitting in her stomach all day like a rock. It didn't matter how confident she was in Beckett's case—fathers rarely got the same grace, even when the truth was clear. Especially when the mother claims to love her child. The injustice of it left a bitter taste in her mouth.

She tried to remain calm, but her thoughts spun through every worst-case scenario. Her appetite vanished hours ago. The clock on her monitor read 4:16 p.m. No call. No text. No video message. And every tick of the clock made the anxiety climb higher.

To distract herself, she started tidying her desk. It was Friday after all, and sorting through old files gave her something to focus on.

By the time she looked up again, the screen read 4:26 p.m. Time was crawling.

Her phone lit up silently—she'd muted it earlier. On the third flash of light, she picked up.

"Miss Vansley is holding on line five," the receptionist said before transferring the call.

While the line clicked and held, Nalexia's mind slipped away again… back to the kiss that changed everything.

That winter night, the cold had wrapped around them like a secret, but all she felt was the warmth of Beckett's arms. His neatly trimmed beard brushed her cheek, then came the softness of his full lips. He pulled her closer, and when she opened to his kiss, it was like time surrendered to them.

A voice broke through her memory. "Can you hear me?"

She blinked back into the present—Miss Vansley was speaking.

"Yes, ma'am," Nalexia replied quickly, flustered. The woman was confirming an appointment for Tuesday. Nalexia checked her calendar and confirmed, then glanced at the time again—4:36 p.m. The workday was done.

The office buzzed with the usual Friday farewells and weekend plans. Her coworker Elle—who insisted on being called *El*, and said it with a thick Boston accent that Nalexia found adorable—popped her head over the cubicle wall.

"Ready?" El asked, already packed up.

Nalexia nodded, shutting down her computer.

There was something about Fridays that made people warmer, friendlier. She smirked at the way the entire office seemed to exhale. As they walked out into the lobby, the sound of heels tapping against polished marble echoed in the open space. Sunlight beamed through the glass entrance, catching the diamond pendant around Nalexia's neck and making it shimmer.

The air was crisp but promising—like the weather couldn't decide if winter was ending or just pausing.

They bypassed the elevators and exited through the rear. As they passed the courtyard, heading toward the parking garage, El slowed down and glanced over at her friend.

"You okay? You seem… off."

Nalexia gave a weak smile. "Just nervous, that's all."

El bumped her shoulder playfully. "You've got nothin' to worry about."

She meant it, even if the odds had always favored the mother. But El had seen it for herself—how terrified Beckett's daughter had been that first night they brought her home. Her tiny body shaking. Her screams at the sound of running water.

After that, El never doubted the fight for full custody again.

Down the cement stairs of the garage, their conversation became light—simple small talk to fill the space. Their cars were parked in the same row, and El spotted Nalexia's white sedan first.

Without warning, El pulled out her phone and hit record.

Something told her this was a moment worth capturing.

Nalexia's breath caught.

Tears pooled in her eyes as she spotted the bouquet resting on the hood of her car. The roses were a stunning blend of fuchsia and crimson, wrapped in a single black silk ribbon—their signature colors. Her fingers trembled as she reached for them, caressing the ribbon like it might whisper to her.

A smile cracked across her face—the first one all day.

She leaned forward and picked up a thick, gleaming envelope, heavy in her hand. The foil shimmered under the garage lights, and on the back, an old-fashioned wax seal with Beckett's initials pressed into the surface.

El cheered from behind the camera, "Girl, open it! Open it!"

Nalexia gave her a look, but the excitement was contagious. She peeled the seal and opened the card slowly, carefully.

You have been understanding, brave, and my source of motivation.

This weekend, I want to take time and focus on you.

The children are fine. We'll see them Monday after work.

Meet me at 3111 Fairview Park Drive. Ask for Kathy at the front desk.

She read the message aloud, her voice cracking with emotion.

El squealed, spinning in a mini-dance. "Yessss! Go, girl! I want *all* the details on Monday!"

With a soft laugh, Nalexia slid into her car. She started the ignition, and Usher's voice poured from the speakers—*"I can make you a believer..."*

She pulled out of the garage slowly, carefully.

As her car emerged into the golden wash of daylight, she slipped on her black rhinestone-dusted sunglasses.

And just like that—joy returned.

For now, the worry was gone.

She didn't give her gut feeling a second thought.

Chapter 2

Elle pulled out of the parking garage, her black Mini Cooper hugging the curb behind Nalexia's car. A sleek, late-model black truck with a matte finish swerved suddenly between them, cutting her off. She slammed on her brakes, heart skipping, then muttered to herself, "Really?"

The truck lingered too long in her path—oddly deliberate—but Elle shrugged it off. It was Friday, and she had her own plans: wine, a blank canvas, and a sip-and-paint night with a few familiar strangers.

By the time she reached Williams Drive, the same black truck was weaving through traffic with increasing aggression. Elle frowned. *Weirdo.* She mentally filed the vehicle under "jerks to avoid" and continued toward the Mosaic District.

Parking near the storefront labeled *Muse*, Elle stepped into the evening air. Spring was being flirtatious—sun-drenched but cool. She glanced at her sundress and flats, then laughed to herself, hearing Nalexia's voice echo in her head: *"You can't wear that dress without a heel. It's against the rules of cuteness."*

Elle opened her trunk and pulled out the gold-toned sandals Nalexia had given her last fall for "Good Friend Day." Nalexia always found reasons to celebrate the people she loved. Just thinking about her made Elle smile—and made her stand taller.

Inside *Muse*, the atmosphere was buzzing with music, chatter, and clinking wine glasses. Her friends were already at the bar, waving her over. They weren't her usual circle. She'd met Cynthia and Todd on a night that had started with a disappointing date and ended with unexpected connections.

Elle had grown fond of them. Cynthia had edge, Todd had energy, and together they had a kind of chaotic charm. As they found their seats for the painting session, the instructor guided them into brush strokes and base colors. Elle began to relax. The black truck faded from her thoughts entirely.

Midway through painting a sky of soft oranges and blues, Todd leaned over. "So, when are you getting back on that dating app?"

Elle rolled her eyes without looking up from her canvas. “Still not a fan.”

“You’re gorgeous, Elle. And your aura screams ‘mysterious and slightly unapproachable.’ That’s dating gold!”

“She likes breathing air that’s not desperate,” Cynthia interrupted with a smirk.

Elle smiled. Cynthia had clearly noticed Todd was overstepping. Moments later, she ordered another round of drinks to redirect the conversation. When they arrived, Elle mouthed a thank you. Cynthia winked and raised her glass in solidarity.

As the class ended, Elle studied her painting—a surprisingly decent beach scene. With another round in hand, they laughed, joked, and dissected their chaotic weeks. But as the evening wore on and Cynthia hit round five of drinks, Elle noticed the mood shift. Todd was now venting about his housing issues, and Cynthia—only half-joking—suggested they move in together. The banter had bite to it. There was history brewing between them.

Then came the moment Elle knew it was time to go: Todd grabbed Cynthia's breast while she was dancing with another guy. Cynthia didn't even flinch. The Afrobeat music thumped through the venue, drowning the discomfort in bass and rhythm.

Elle slipped out quietly.

The air was cooler now, the sun finally tucking behind the horizon. She didn't feel like going straight home. A craving for coffee nudged her toward the upscale grocery store around the corner.

Inside, she wandered aimlessly—past overpriced granola, imported jams, and curated cheeses. She didn't really need anything but walked anyway, letting the movement help her sober up.

She passed the milk aisle but turned toward the housewares instead. Wine glasses. Scented candles. Mugs with phrases like *"You've got this"* and *"Self-care is sacred."*

That's when the thought hit her: *I think Nalexia's getting engaged this weekend.*

Elle had known Nalexia since they were girls playing double dutch behind their elementary school. She'd seen her friend rise, fall, grieve, survive, and now thrive. The career. The child. The man. And soon, maybe a ring.

For a moment, standing between silicone baking mats and copper measuring cups, Elle felt a pang she hadn't expected. Not resentment—just… absence. A soft ache for something she couldn't quite name.

It's her time, Elle told herself.

But the feeling lingered, just beneath the surface.

And somewhere, on a back road, a black truck turned into the darkness.

Chapter 3

Nalexia typed the address from Beckett's card into her GPS and was surprised to find it was just five minutes from her office. As she turned into the circular drive, the gold Marriott sign gleamed above her, catching the late-afternoon light. A valet in a crisp black uniform approached her window.

"Good evening, miss. Any bags tonight?"

Nalexia smiled shyly. "No, just me."

He nodded, offering her a warm grin and a claim ticket with a subtle Caribbean accent lacing his words. She thanked him and stepped out of the car, her heels clicking on the smooth stone driveway.

The oversized glass doors opened automatically as she approached, and the moment she stepped inside, she felt transported. Cream marble floors shimmered beneath crystal lighting. The lobby was a symphony of elegance: oversized couches in neutral tones, cathedral ceilings, and a sweeping mahogany reception desk that anchored the space.

A couple sat at the nearby lounge sipping wine, lost in quiet conversation. It reminded her of Beckett, and a flutter of anticipation stirred in her chest.

She moved slowly, drinking in every detail—the texture of the walls, the play of light against the polished surfaces, the curated artwork. Beauty. She had always noticed it. Loved it. Sought it.

Three attendants stood behind the front desk, each helping guests. Nalexia waited patiently, her fingers brushing the strap of her purse.

Finally, a blonde woman at the far end looked up with a smile. "Hi there. How can I help you?"

"I'm here for Beckett Landsburg's reservation," Nalexia said, then added, "Actually, I was told to ask for Kathy?"

The blonde's smile deepened like she was in on a secret. "Kathy's on break, but I've got you." She tapped a few keys. "Looks like everything's been taken care of."

With an almost giddy sweetness in her voice, the attendant slid a key card across the counter along with a sleek envelope and two spa passes.

"There you go, Ms. Nalexia. Elevators are to your left—past the corridor with the gold inlay floor tiles."

Nalexia thanked her, genuinely touched by the warm welcome, and followed the directions. The hallway shimmered with elegance—the marble tile broken by gilded brass lines that led the way like a runway. She paused at the elevators, four sets of polished brass doors gleaming under the overhead lights.

One opened, revealing two young women in club-ready outfits, all heels and high energy. Nalexia chuckled softly. The hotel must have a bar—or maybe a secret party she didn't know about.

She stepped into the now-empty elevator. Just as the doors began to close, a thin man slipped in, tall and angular, with a scruffy beard. He stood near the controls.

"Which floor?"

"Seven, please."

He pressed the button, then glanced at her. "Pretty voice," he said. "Be careful out there. Gotta watch out for crazies."

She smiled politely, thinking nothing of it.

But as the elevator came to a stop and Nalexia stepped out, the man leaned down, dropped a wireless microphone into her oversized purse, and let the doors close behind her.

Unaware, Nalexia continued, following the plush carpet down two quiet corners. The navy-blue wallpaper and soft lighting gave the hall a royal, intimate feel. Room 724. She slid the card key into the slot. A red light. Then green.

The door clicked open.

Rose petals carpeted the floor in soft waves of color. The same rich fuchsia and crimson as the bouquet on her car. At the far end of the room, Beckett lounged on a chaise, his baritone voice curling toward her like smoke.

"So… how was your day?"

Nalexia broke into a wide smile. “It was stressful,” she teased. “Some guy that I like ghosted me all day. Had me worried sick.”

Beckett chuckled from the chaise. “Sounds like you should drop him, for me.”

She tilted her head, playing coy. “You want me to leave him, for you?”

Without hesitation: “Yep.”

They laughed. The joke was one they shared often—pretending to be each other’s forbidden fling and forever lover all at once. He reminded her again, in that voice that always unraveled her, that he was whatever she needed—husband, friend, lover—as long as it was *him*.

He stood and walked toward her.

Nalexia held his gaze, her body humming with desire. She stepped back until her spine pressed against the cool wallpapered wall. Beckett’s hands found her hips, grounding her.

“Stand on your toes,” he whispered.

She obeyed, her breath catching as he spun her gently. His hands slid down her legs, pausing at her ankles before gliding slowly up the soft skin of her calf, then her inner thigh. She braced herself against the wall, bending slightly.

When his fingers found the damp heat of her center through her panties, he groaned low in his throat. “I’ve been waiting *all* day to do this.” His hushed tone was filled with desire.

He teased her with deliberate strokes—slow, maddening. When she was trembling, he abruptly stopped. With one motion, he lifted her dress over her hips, exposing her lilac lace panties.

“Are these new?” he asked.

A breathy, “Yes,” was all she could manage.

Her legs shook from arousal and the strain of standing on tiptoe. Beckett adjusted her stance, bending her forward, her palms flat on the wall. He freed himself, his desire thick and urgent, and thrust into her from behind.

The purse fell to the floor with a soft thud. Forgotten.

Each movement of his hips was precise, powerful. Nalexia moaned, her voice reverent—thankful. She whispered his name like a prayer and thanked God aloud for the pleasure blooming through her.

Just when she thought she was close, Beckett unzipped her dress and let it fall to the floor. He kissed the curve of her back, then dropped to his knees again, worshipping her with his mouth—his tongue tracing circles between her thighs, slipping even further. She gasped, her coos melting into soft cries of release.

Then he was inside her again.

Their rhythm returned, slow and intentional. Her body trembled with the approach of climax. He knew. He guided her with his hands, his strokes deep and unrelenting until her body exploded in a shivering wave of release.

Only then did he let go.

He gripped her hips tighter, buried himself deeper, and spilled everything he had—every drop, every promise.

They spent the rest of the weekend wrapped in each other's laughter, love, and sweat.

They binged Netflix, made love in intervals, and only paused long enough for Beckett to feed her—because Nalexia was entirely focused on *him*.

On Sunday evening, Nalexia curled against him, her voice soft. "How did it go?"

Beckett's smile faded into something solemn, laced with relief and sadness.

"The judge granted me sole custody… temporarily. It gives her time to get herself together."

Nalexia listened quietly as he recounted how Kimmy had unraveled in the courtroom—yelling, crying, needing to be escorted out. And worst of all, their daughter had seen it all.

Nalexia's heart ached—not for Kimmy, but for the little girl who just needed love… and safety.

And as the room dimmed with the setting sun, Nalexia held Beckett tighter, knowing the road ahead wouldn't be easy—but certain they'd face it together.

Chapter 4

A soft but frustrated voice pierced the early evening air in the parking lot of Beckett's warehouse.

"What do you mean it won't be ready for me to listen to until tomorrow?" the woman snapped, standing just out of view behind a delivery van.

Bosco, the janitor, paused mid-push with his trash can. The wheels creaked as he slowed down, listening. He wasn't trying to be nosey, but something about her tone made him uneasy. She wasn't yelling, but her voice carried the weight of entitlement—and impatience. Whoever she was, she didn't sound like she belonged in a place like this, especially after hours.

The warehouse lot was mostly empty. Only a few vehicles remained—mostly staff staying late to finish inventory or review security protocols. Bosco glanced over the van, catching only the back of the woman's sleek black coat as she climbed into a dark sedan. Her face remained hidden. The car rolled away slowly, the sound of tires whispering over gravel.

Moments later, Mitchell emerged from the side entrance of the warehouse, walking briskly toward the lot with a file folder in hand and his phone to his ear. His eyes scanned the space, narrowing as he spotted Bosco standing still near the trash bins.

"You good, B?" Mitchell asked, ending the call and tucking the folder under his arm.

Bosco hesitated, then shrugged. "Yeah, I'm good. Just… something weird. Some woman was out here just now, arguing with someone over the phone. It sounded like she was expecting to hear something—audio, maybe?"

Mitchell's expression shifted slightly, curiosity ignited. "You recognize her?"

"No. Never seen her before. But she wasn't just hanging out. She was pissed about something."

Mitchell nodded slowly, tapping the edge of the file against his thigh. The timing was suspicious. Just last week, Beckett had discovered a minor security breach—nothing stolen, but the system had been tampered with. Now, someone was lurking around the property after hours?

"Alright," Mitchell said. "Thanks for letting me know, Bosco. If you see her again—or anyone unfamiliar—snap a photo, alright?"

Bosco nodded. "Will do."

Mitchell turned and walked back toward the warehouse, the weight of the file in his hand suddenly feeling heavier. Inside were specs for Beckett's upcoming launch—the moon-powered generator, the crown jewel of their clean tech initiative.

He'd been trying to downplay the breach to Beckett, chalking it up to a system glitch. But now his gut told him otherwise.

Someone was watching.

And they weren't watching for fun.

Chapter 5

Beckett was no stranger to long hours. Twelve-hour stretches often passed unnoticed—especially on days when Kimmy showed up. On those days, he buried himself in his work, hoping exhaustion would erase the urge to shake some sense into her. The last thing his daughter needed was her father behind bars for losing control.

Outside Beckett's office, the massive bay door let in a gust of warm air. Bosco pushed his rolling cart inside from the lot. Beckett noticed him from the corner of his eye—how the old man lingered, clearly wanting to say something but unsure how.

Bosco shuffled into the office, grabbed the trash bin without a word, and disappeared again. He returned moments later, breaking down cardboard boxes for recycling. Still silent.

Beckett never questioned Bosco's habit of collecting scrap parts from the production floor. Everyone assumed the old janitor had a secret side project—maybe building something useful or quirky at home. Beckett always figured one day Bosco would surprise them with something he could actually market.

Beckett stood then left his office, heading to one of the engineering bays where a final demonstration was being prepped. It was a prototype of a solar generator designed to pull limited energy from lunar reflections. Bosco followed, keeping a respectful distance.

The room buzzed with anticipation. Engineers were adjusting components, while a camera team captured the entire process. Each final demo was recorded for investor presentations.

Mitchell—Beckett's right-hand and warehouse production manager—stood at his side, stylus in hand, ready to jot down anything Beckett said. He admired Beckett almost like a little brother would—awe and loyalty wrapped in productivity.

Beckett paced slowly around the device, hands in his pockets. "It's got to look sleek," he said. "Can we make it faster? Cheaper to build? Better looking?"

The engineers fumbled to respond. It wasn't a challenge. It was a standard, Beckett pushed—to make them think bigger.

In less than ten minutes, the team had reimagined the casing and shaved costs on materials. Beckett gave a small approving smile and walked off. Mitchell lingered behind, praising their pivot.

Beckett's mind returned to business strategy. It was never just about supply and demand. He wanted to create tools that made life better—for less. Each invention was a love letter to possibility.

His passion was born young, back when he worked as a helper handing out supplies to real engineers. One man—Docket, affectionately called "Doc"—took him under his wing and taught him the anatomy of an idea. From concept to creation, then to corporate pitching. Doc was now retired, but Beckett still sent him supplies and even brokered deals to keep his mentor's retirement comfortable. Doc wasn't just a mentor—he was the father Beckett never had.

Back in Beckett''s office, Mitchell returned. "Boss, do you want me to send today's test footage to your tablet?"

Beckett glanced at his watch, surprised by the time. His stomach dropped. *He hadn't heard from Nalexia all day.*

"Mitch, have I missed any calls?"

Mitchell pressed a button on his smartwatch. "Nylia?"

The voice of their cheerful receptionist came through the tiny speaker. "Yes, Mr. Mitchell?"

"Any missed calls for Beckett today?"

Keys clacked in the background, then a pause. "Mmm… nope. No missed calls logged. Need anything else before I head out?"

Beckett answered himself. "Thanks, Nylia. Have a good night."

His fingers patted around his desk, searching. "Where's my phone?"

Mitchell joined the search.

Just as Beckett began to panic, Bosco entered again. Beckett turned sharply. "Bosco, you've been trying to say something all day. Just spit it out."

His tone was cold, but Bosco didn't flinch.

"I know that woman from earlier was your daughter's mother…"

Mitchell glanced up from the floor. "Still going straight to voicemail."

Beckett locked eyes with Bosco, silently giving permission to continue.

Bosco's voice was uneven. "You need to keep an eye on that girl. That's all I wanted to say."

Mitchell suddenly straightened. "Found it!"

The phone was dead. Beckett plugged it in—and when it powered up, thirteen missed calls and five text messages flooded the screen.

All from his son.

His heart thudded.

Each text from Bradley was more urgent than the last.

Beckett called immediately. The phone barely rang before his son answered. In the background, a woman's voice spoke—soft, but unmistakably familiar.

"What's going on?" Beckett barked.

"Dad," Bradley started, "she demanded to drive me home from practice. I told her I could walk, but she followed me. She had Charlotte with her."

Charlotte. His four-year-old daughter.

Beckett's fury burned—but he kept his voice calm. "Okay, son. I'm sorry I missed your calls. My phone died. I'm on my way now."

Bradley brightened. "Can I talk to you while you drive?"

Beckett smiled at his son's attempt to stall time. "I'd love that, but let me make a few quick calls. I'll see you in a bit, alright?"

As he ended the call, Mitchell re-entered. "You good, Boss?"

Beckett nodded. "I'm straight."

Bosco, still nearby, gave a grin. "Hardest working young man I've ever seen."

Beckett packed his bag with his essentials: Beats headphones, tablet, cords, laptop. He grabbed his blazer from the coat rack and slung his black leather messenger bag over one shoulder.

As he reached the warehouse door, his phone vibrated again. It was a message from Nalexia:

I love you. Completely.

A soft smile tugged at Beckett's lips.

Bosco caught it. "How's my girl doing?"

Beckett chuckled. "She's good."

"Sweet girl," Bosco said, then added with a playful grin, "Sweet enough to eat!"

Beckett laughed. "Watch it, Old Man. I'll lay hands on you quick if you get fresh."

The two men shared a laugh as Beckett stepped outside.

He climbed into his car, started the engine, and immediately called Nalexia.

Chapter 6

"Hey, handsome."

Nalexia's voice came through the car speakers before the Bluetooth connected fully, making Beckett smile even harder than he already was. Just hearing her made everything feel lighter. She asked about his day, and Beckett told her everything—Kimmy's rant, her unexpected approach to Bradley on his walk home, and how it had rattled him. They talked the whole way to his house, a habit that had grown into something neither of them wanted to break. Big things, small things—everything felt worth sharing now.

Nalexia had sensed Beckett needed to refocus on his kids after the new custody agreement. Without needing to say much, she gave him space—but still stayed close, always just a call away.

The next few days were long. Beckett worked eight-hour shifts at the warehouse, then another four hours in the evening after spending time with Bradley and Charlotte. Kimmy was supposed to see Charlotte midweek, but the night before, she canceled.

Said she was dealing with "life stuff." She didn't mention she was quietly researching ways to manipulate custody again—to squeeze more money from Beckett once things shifted in her favor.

But Beckett didn't let her absence throw him off. He adapted quickly, reorganized his schedule, and kept moving forward.

Finally, the work paid off.

He had a series of inventions ready for presentation—one in particular, the moon-powered generator, had generated buzz before it was even demoed. Buyers were already lined up. Mitchell, who'd never attended a demo with actual investors before, was pumped.

The demonstration lab was pristine. Bright, white walls glowed under overhead lighting. Arrows on the floor directed guests to sleek, stone seating areas. The receptionist, Nylia, handed out crisp information packets while engineers and their families filled in. Beckett had invited Nalexia and Doc. He was proud—this was his world, and he wanted them in it.

Across the room, he caught Nalexia's eye and smiled. The look she gave him made his chest warm. She supported him. She cared. Kimmy, by contrast, had never once shown interest in his work. Not like this.

The demonstration began. Beckett stepped onto the plexiglass platform, introduced the product model, and explained how the moon-powered generator worked—in simple language that even a child could grasp. The model performed flawlessly. During the Q&A, Beckett handled every question with precision and charm.

By the end of the night, he'd sold nearly half a million units.Mitchell was blown away. He finally understood why the engineers were loyal to Beckett—it wasn't just the vision. Beckett had built a model where inventors could thrive creatively and still profit. That was rare.

Mitchell and Nylia gathered the orders. Mitchell had already set up a follow-up meeting with the tech team for the next morning. Mass production would begin immediately.

As the night wound down, Doc invited the team to a family-owned Italian restaurant off

Old Branch Avenue. Beckett gave his head of security strict orders on locking down the lab and scanning the premises before heading out.

Outside, just as everyone was piling into cars, Nalexia glanced down.

"Oh shoot—I think I left my purse."

She turned and jogged back toward the lab. Inside, the white glow of the lab was dimmer, shadows pressing against corners. As she neared the chairs, she caught a glimpse of something—or someone. A figure near the exit on the far end of the lab. An older man. Her pulse jumped. She squinted, trying to place him.

"The elevator man", she said in a disbelieving whisper. The same man from the Marriott two weeks ago. She moved closer hesitantly. By the time she crossed the room, the door on the opposite side of the showroom was locked, no one was there.

Maybe she was mistaken. The warehouse did look different at night.

"Honey?" Beckett's voice echoed behind her. He'd come back inside. "Did you find your purse?"

Nalexia nodded. “I did. But... I could’ve sworn I saw someone walk out the far door.”

She pointed. Beckett looked serious now. “Security will sweep the whole place before locking down,” he promised. But he made a mental note to double-check that door himself. Whoever she saw—or thought she saw—might not have been random. But for now, he just wanted to enjoy the night.

Outside, a driver pulled up in a sleek black SUV and whisked them to the restaurant. Doc had reserved a private room in the back, and the team celebrated with wine, pasta, and laughter.

Still, Beckett couldn’t shake what Nalexia said.

And somewhere, on the edges of that bright, beautiful night, something dark had already slipped through the door.

Chapter 7

Monday morning came with sharp edges that sliced through the remnants of the weekend's calm. Beckett's alarm hadn't even buzzed before he was up, dressed in a black hoodie and slacks, standing in his home office, scanning footage from Saturday night. The glow from the screen illuminated the lines of worry etched on his forehead as Nalexia's words echoed louder now in the quiet—"I swear I saw someone leave through that back door." And Beckett believed her.

By 7:00 a.m., he was at the warehouse, the gentle warmth of spring wrapping around him as he stepped out of his car, an almost deceptive comfort against the heaviness in his heart.

Mitchell arrived next, carrying two coffees, the steam curling into the air like whispers of comfort, already sensing Beckett's mood. "Rough night?" he asked, but Beckett didn't answer. He just nodded toward the surveillance room, the weight of unspoken tension heavy between them.

Inside, Mitchell had already queued up the interior and exterior camera feeds from the night of the demonstration. Beckett stood behind him, arms folded tightly across his chest, eyes laser-focused, as if willing the truth to reveal itself. The flickering screens cast shadows on their faces, mirroring the unease brewing within.

It wasn't long before they spotted it.

"Pause that," Beckett commanded, his voice steady despite the racing heart in his chest.

The feed froze on a shadow moving across the back corridor—no badge, no name tag, and no face caught fully on camera. The door Nalexia mentioned clicked open, just wide enough for someone to slip out, a fleeting moment captured in time.

Beckett leaned in, breath hitching. "Back it up."

Mitchell rewound. They slowed it. Frame by frame, the tension in the room thickened. A tall man, hooded, quick-footed, moved like he belonged—but he didn't.

"Looks like the guy from the Nissan dealer when I took Nalexia's car in for an oil change a few weeks back," Mitchell muttered, his eyes narrowing in recognition. "Same build. Same walk."

"Same MO," Beckett added, his gut twisting with a sense of dread. They didn't need full confirmation. Beckett knew when something smelled off—and this wasn't just off. It was layered. Layered with intent, like a storm brewing on the horizon.

Meanwhile, Nalexia sat at home, swirling creamer into her tea as she gazed at the floor-to-ceiling glass door off her balcony. The area in her reading nook was usually comforting, but now the silence amplified her uneasiness. Something inside her buzzed—a gut feeling she'd learned to respect over time. She wasn't scared exactly, but the peace she'd fought for felt… fragile. The pressure building behind it was palpable, an impending storm threatening to break.

Beckett hadn't texted her that morning. Not even a simple "good morning" or a coffee emoji.

She picked up her phone, fingers trembling as she typed.

Nalexia: "*Everything okay over there?*"

Five minutes passed, the ticking clock echoing her rising anxiety.

Then her screen lit up.

Beckett: "Come to the warehouse. Bring your car. Don't ask why yet."

The urgency in his text message, the words sent a shiver down her spine. She canceled her afternoon meetings.

By the time Nalexia arrived, the sun hung low in the sky, casting long shadows across the parking lot. Beckett was already waiting, a tense silhouette against the fading light, accompanied by a man she didn't recognize. He was strikingly handsome, with a head full of large, loose curls that framed a serious expression. He looked ex-military, with a laptop in one hand and what appeared to be a wand in the other—an unsettling combination of beauty and danger.

"Tyger," Beckett introduced, his voice low. "My childhood best friend and silent partner. He's here to sweep your car."

Nalexia's brow lifted, confusion mingling with apprehension. "Sweep?" She had spent time with Tyger before but he usually stayed in the shadows watching everything from a distance.

“For trackers. Or bugs.”

Her breath caught, a lump forming in her throat. “Beckett…”

“I believe you. About the man at the event demo. I think he’s been following you. Or us.”

Tyger opened her car doors, methodically scanning the vehicle with a handheld detector. It buzzed faintly when he reached beneath the driver's seat, the sound cutting through the tension like a knife.

“Got something,” he grunted, pulling out a small black device—no bigger than a thumb drive. Beckett’s heart raced, heat rising in his chest as he took one look.

“This isn’t amateur tech,” Tyger said, his tone grave. “Military grade. Someone spent real money for this.”

Nalexia’s hand flew to her mouth, the reality crashing down around her. “Is it tracking me?”

“Yes,” Beckett answered, his voice steady but filled with an undercurrent of fury before Tyger could respond. “And recording us.”

He walked a few paces away, fists clenched at his sides. The attack wasn’t loud—but it was personal. Quiet. Creeping. Calculated.

He turned back to her, emotion flooding his voice. “From now on, we don’t assume privacy. Not in your car. Not on your phone. I’ve already had my office swept. Mitchell and Bosco are the only ones briefed.”

Nalexia stepped closer, her voice low, calm, but firm. “Beckett… who would do this?” As her question left her full luscious lips, the same alerting noise came from Tyger’s meter. Everyone in Beckett's office froze. Tyger placed his finger over his lips, expressing the “shh” sound to explain for everyone to stop talking and allow him to listen. He waved the wand over Nalexia, searching over her head down to her shoes. There was nothing, but when the wand got close to her purse, there seemed to be a beep from the wand alerting them that there was another tracking device. Beckett snatched the purse off the desk and dumped its contents. Nalexia's personal items crashed down on top of the desk: her wallet, loose change, Chapstick, hand sanitizer, cell phone, hand lotion, a bottle of travel-size perfume, a hairbrush, a few extra hair scrunchies, vitamins, and even her iPad rested on the top of the pile. On the very top of the pile was some type of device, a little larger than a thumb drive, that had Bluetooth capability on the side.

“How long have you been carrying this particular bag? I know how women are; I know you all switch bags all the time. When was the last time you used this bag?” Tyger’s question was very demanding and intense. Beckett stood and waited for Nalexia to respond.

“I used this purse the same weekend that Beckett surprised me after work. Today was the first time that I've used it since then.”

“Someone who doesn’t want me to win.”

She inhaled sharply, brows furrowing as she grasped the gravity of their situation. “Or someone who doesn’t want us to win.”

Back inside the warehouse, the atmosphere thickened with urgency as Beckett, Mitchell, and Tyger reviewed security logs, the glow of the screens casting ghostly shadows on their faces. They began rebuilding new protocols—biometric upgrades, rotating access codes, limited entry points. Beckett even pulled Doc in on a secure call, laying out the details piece by piece.

"If it's corporate espionage, they're trying to steal designs," Doc said, his voice steady yet filled with an edge of concern.

"If it's personal," Beckett replied, the weight of the implications heavy in the air, "they're using her to get to me."

Doc fell silent for a long moment, the tension palpable. Finally, he said, "Either way, you need to prepare for war."

That night, after the warehouse cleared, Beckett sat alone in the demo lab, lights dimmed, watching replays of the weekend's celebration. The laughter, the innovation, and the warmth of Nalexia's hand on his thigh—all of it felt real. But now, it was shadowed by the threat looming over them.

He opened his phone, scrolling past Kimmy's latest string of missed calls, past text messages from investors, past the warehouse updates—each notification a reminder of the life he'd fought to build.

And finally, he opened the one video security hadn't yet decrypted—the silent, grainy clip of the Marriott elevator. There he was. The same man. The same eyes that flickered toward Nalexia when she stepped off the elevator that night, a predator lurking in the shadows. Beckett stared at the screen, jaw clenched, fury igniting within him. Then he whispered to himself, words laced with a resolve that echoed in the empty lab: "You made this personal."

And personal… meant there were no limits.

Chapter 8

Twenty minutes later, Kimmy arrived at Seth's luxury hotel suite.

He was a smooth-talking real estate developer her sister had introduced her to—charming, well-dressed, and in town pursuing a new investment project. They had been seeing each other off and on, though Kimmy had always kept things casual. But tonight, she was desperate.

The moment the door closed behind her, Kimmy pushed her body into his. She didn't wait for sweet talk. Seth didn't ask questions. He didn't care. He never did. He spun her around, bent her over the table, and held her down with one hand pressed firmly to her neck. The cold glass surface kissed her cheek. With the other hand, Seth tore open a condom with his teeth and used his foot to spread her legs wider.

Kimmy didn't flinch.

A single tear fell down her cheek.

Seth never noticed. He was fighting his own inner battles that she never asked about because Kimmy rarely asked about the men she dealt with. Her daddy issues always rose to the surface and blocked the human quality of men.

She wasn't crying because of what he was doing—but because of everything he wasn't. She thought about the audio recording of Nalexia she'd secretly played on repeat. Nalexia's moans, breathless and full of life. Kimmy was wet just remembering it. But no man—not even now—had ever made her sound like that nor feel how she imagined Nalexia must have felt to let out such climatic moans. The seed of desire to be Nalexia had been planted and the recording watered that desire.

Seth finished with a grunt, disappeared into the bathroom, and flushed the condom like a routine chore. Kimmy remained still. Numb.

The ache wasn't physical—it was emotional. A hollow sadness she couldn't shake. "*Why doesn't sex ever feel good for me? The longing to be able to feel grew.*"

She shoved the thought down. Just like always.

When Seth came back out, he casually placed an Uber Eats order and collapsed onto the couch. Kimmy wandered to his open work binder, a combination of portfolio work that he completed projects he was hoping to be a part of and flipped through glossy protective sheet covered documents full of high-end properties and lucrative projects. A younger Seth smiled up at her from a photo tucked inside—his arm around a pretty girl.

Kimmy lifted the photo with a smirk. "So who's this?" she teased, fanning the picture like a playing card. Usually she would not care but the girl in the picture was the girl version of the women she would trade places with. "Most people keep their exes on their phones, not in binders."

Seth glanced up, completely unfazed. "That's me and the one that got away." Kimmy hated that his words stung.

He said it like it was nothing, but as he kept talking, his tone softened.

"She was young. I was stupid. Things were good—*really* good. I started to catch feelings, and when she told me she was pregnant, I told her to call the other guy she was messing with and get it handled." His voice cracked with an unspoken regret.

Seth's thoughts wandered to the younger version of himself. The unsure individual, he intentionally dated younger women because he needed to position himself to be the source of pleasure that boys their own age had not yet learned to provide. Kimmy missed that. Kimmy missed all the nuances that Seth did.

Kimmy didn't blink, focused only on the girl from the picture. "What was her name?"

She knew already. But she needed him to say it.

"Nalexia," Seth breathed, like the word had its own gravitational pull.

Kimmy's jaw tensed. "*This bitch keeps popping up", she mumbled to herself.*

Even Seth? Kimmy's eyes rolled in disbelief. Nalexia had even taken *him* from her.

Playing it cool, Kimmy leaned in with a smile. "You should reach out. See how life's treating her. Can't hurt."

Seth looked down, pensive. "Keolani told me she's not married. Still in property management." A slow grin spread across his face.

Kimmy watched it happen—watched him fall back in time.

And in her silence, she started doing math in her head. Maybe she could become Nalexia. Or at least a version of what Beckett wanted. If it meant stability… or a few more dollars… she could play along. She could help Seth rekindle. She considered what was in it for her to help Seth. She hated being a single mom. And she never realized how much Beckett had truly provided until he wasn't around anymore.

They cuddled that night. Watching movies. Both pretending the other was someone else.

The next morning, Kimmy slipped out before sunrise.

She used the gym bathroom across from her job to freshen up—a quick "hoe bath," as she called it—then clocked into work at the salon.

The day was slow. She didn't mind. The job didn't fulfill her, but it gave her just enough of what she needed: a paycheck that let her legally keep needing Beckett—and avoid moving back into her father's house.

Today, she was allowed to pick up Charlotte.

Her lawyer had negotiated a court amendment: one full week with her daughter, if she showed progress. A job, was progress. But she had to stay at a court-approved location during the week—either her sister's or her father's. That clause burned her pride.

Still, it had been three weeks since she'd seen Charlotte. Kimmy wasn't about to blow it.

She pulled into the daycare parking lot, took a breath, and walked in.

At the front desk, the receptionist smiled and handed her the sign-out sheet. "Just need your signature, Mom. We'll call for Charlotte."

Kimmy glanced around, surprised. The center had undergone a complete makeover. Fresh paint. Upgraded equipment. Security cameras.

“I see y’all have made some upgrades,” Kimmy commented, trying not to sneer.

“Oh yes,” the receptionist beamed. “Thanks to Mr. Landsburg. He really blessed us. We’ve got Smart Boards in every room, new vans for field trips, even engineering equipment for the older kids. He’s amazing.”

Kimmy’s stomach turned.

Beckett again.

His logo was etched in glass near the classroom door: *Inventors & Inventions.*

Of course. Always the hero. Always the good guy.

Inside Charlotte’s class, Kimmy ripped her daughter’s coat and backpack from the hook. Her movements were sharp and aggressive. Even the kids noticed. The teacher’s smile dropped.

“Is everything alright?” she asked gently.

Kimmy glared. “Everything’s just fine.”

She stormed out, Charlotte on her hip. The teacher followed her to the hallway and stopped at the reception desk.

"I think we need to call Mr. Landsburg," the teacher said, voice low but urgent. "This is her first pickup under the new court order, and… something felt off."

The receptionist tried Beckett's number. "No answer. But I do have instructions to contact the caseworker if anything unusual happens. Should we?"

The teacher paused.

Outside, Kimmy buckled Charlotte into the back seat, feeling the heat of eyes still watching her. She turned to the glass doors, glared through them, and mouthed the word:

Bitch.

That was all the teacher needed to pick up the phone. And file a report.

Chapter 9

Kimmy pulled away from the daycare with Charlotte in the back seat, her tiny sobs filling the silence.

"Can I call Daddy?" Charlotte asked, sniffling.

"No," Kimmy said curtly. That one word shattered the child's routine—and her composure.

"I want my daddy!" Charlotte wailed. "I *need* to call my daddy!" Her small body shook with tears, and Kimmy's grip on the steering wheel tightened. She kept her eyes on the road, trying to tune it out—but she couldn't.

Overwhelming thoughts in her head... What kind of mother can't soothe her own child? What if I'm not fit to be her mom? What if Nalexia is better at that than me?

The question echoed loud in her head. Her mind drifted, uninvited, to her own mother—distant, cold, never enough. And now, here she was… becoming the same.

Emotion took over. Kimmy tapped the screen on her dashboard and called Beckett. The ring buzzed through the car speakers.

Charlotte immediately quieted.

But when the voicemail picked up, Kimmy panicked and hung up. She didn't want Beckett to hear his daughter's sobs and think something was seriously wrong—or worse, use it against her.

She tried calling again later. No answer.

By the time Kimmy arrived at her sister Kortney's house, Charlotte had wiped her tears but hadn't let go of her frustration.

As Kortney walked through the door, Charlotte rushed her and clung to her waist like a lifeline. Kimmy stood by the threshold, impatient.

"Kortney, can you call Beck from your phone?" Kimmy asked, arms crossed.

Kortney still had bags in her hands. "Hi sweet girl," she said softly to Charlotte. "Help me put these groceries away, and then we'll call your dad and tell him all about your day."

Charlotte nodded eagerly and took a bag with a loaf of bread to the kitchen. Kimmy watched—speechless.

It had never occurred to her to simply talk to Charlotte like that… like a person.

She watched her daughter light up. She saw her confidence. Her intelligence. Her joy. For the first time in a long time, Kimmy felt a flicker of pride—tainted by guilt. "Was any of that even because of me?", she whispered

Charlotte moved easily around the kitchen, putting groceries where they belonged. "At first, the best part of my day was making cake balls during art," she said proudly. "But then Mommy came to get me—and *that* was the best part."

Kimmy smiled.

Kortney caught it, smiled back, and asked gently, "What was the worst part of your day?"

But Charlotte answered before she could finish. "When Mommy had a tantrum and scared my friends."

Kimmy's smile dropped. "Charlotte! You will not disrespect me!" she barked, her voice sharp enough to freeze the room.

Kortney stepped in quickly. "Let's call your dad."

Charlotte sulked and picked up her toy. "Do you think he'll come get me?" she asked, eyes down.

Kortney crouched. "You want to leave before we even make dinner?"

That shifted everything. Charlotte paused. "What are we making?"

"Pigs in a blanket, sweet potato fries… and fresh lemonade," Kortney replied, pulling out ingredients from the bag.

Charlotte clapped. "Can we have broccoli too?!"

Kortney laughed. "Of course we can."

Dinner came together like magic. Charlotte danced around the kitchen. Kimmy stayed mostly quiet, helping when her daughter allowed it. She was beginning to realize—Charlotte wasn't a baby anymore. She was growing up. Fast.

That night, after dinner and a bubble bath, Kimmy used Kortney's phone to call Beckett again.

He picked up on the first ring.

Kimmy said nothing at first—but inside, it stung. Beckett had ignored *her* all day. But for Charlotte? Immediate.

She was learning fast that her usual outbursts had no place with this new version of her daughter.

Once Charlotte was in bed, Kortney handed Kimmy a glass of pink Moscato.

"Why are you so good at being a mom?" Kimmy asked.

Kortney laughed. "I'm not a mom, remember? I'm the aunt. No pressure to get everything right. I just take it moment by moment."

Kimmy swirled her wine, silently taking that in.

Then Kortney probed, "When was the last time you talked to Seth?"

Kimmy didn't respond at first. She took a deep sip. Then another.

"I was with him last night," she finally said, voice flat.

Kortney raised a brow. "What's wrong? You said that like it was… nothing."

Kimmy met her sister's gaze. For the first time in a long time, she saw concern—not judgment.

"Seth's fine. He's probably a great guy. But the last few weeks have been hell. Beckett wins custody. The investigator I hired couldn't find the money I *know* he's hiding. But they *did* find a sex tape—of him. Just my luck. Not helpful for my case."

Kortney winced.

"And to top it off…" Kimmy let out a bitter laugh. "Seth used to date *her*."

Kortney sat up straighter. "Wait—Seth dated who?"

Kimmy unlocked her phone and pulled up a photo. Seth, younger, with Nalexia in his arms. Smiling. Happy.

Kortney stared at the screen. Then downed the rest of her wine. "Damn. It's a small world."

Kimmy stayed in her head after that. Silent. Distant.

Kortney stood. "I've got work early. Goodnight, sis."

"Goodnight," Kimmy murmured.

The rest of the week was rough.

Charlotte and Kimmy struggled to find their rhythm. Kortney helped wherever she could, but Kimmy quickly realized—full-time parenting was no joke. Beckett had made it look easy with the help of a nanny, a flexible job, and money. All Kimmy had was shampooing heads for tips—and a looming deadline.

By Friday, she was drained. She gladly dropped Charlotte off at school, needing the break.

That afternoon, her lawyer left a voicemail. The deadline to appeal the child support ruling was approaching fast. Kimmy had less than a month to make her case—or walk away with less than she thought she deserved.

She stared out the window, her mind racing.

She and Beckett had never married.

Charlotte was all she had left to keep him connected—and keep being provided for.

But time was running out.

And Charlotte?

Charlotte was growing. Watching. Learning.

Soon, Kimmy wouldn't be able to manipulate her either.

Chapter 10

Kimmy had Charlotte for a full week. For Beckett, it was the first time in months he'd had uninterrupted time to himself—and he used it wisely. Long hours at work, investor meetings, new prototypes. But tonight?

Tonight was *for her.*

A date night with Nalexia. Long overdue. Long anticipated. And still, Nalexia worried something would ruin it.

Sitting in her white Nissan Sentra, Nalexia tapped mascara onto her lashes and smoothed on a deep nude lipstick. Her mind wouldn't rest.

Choice—her son—was with her best friend Elle. He had asthma, and the weather had been unpredictable.

Bradley, Beckett's son, was home with Doc—Beckett's old mentor. Doc had no grandchildren of his own, so time with Bradley was special.

Then there was *Charlotte*. And, inevitably, Kimmy.

Nalexia didn't know Kimmy personally, only through the war stories Beckett had shared and the chaos she'd seen up close. What always unsettled her was how *entirely dependent* Kimmy had been on Beckett—housing, groceries, internet, cable, and a live-in nanny who doubled as a housekeeper. Beckett covered it all. And Kimmy still managed to complain.

When Kimmy fired the nanny for reporting too much back to Beckett, he found out that weekends had devolved into Charlotte being babysat by sketchy neighbors in the building. That was the beginning of the end.

Nalexia had never judged Kimmy outright. She knew motherhood was hard. She also knew losing custody would break her. Still, it was Beckett who did the heavy lifting. Who made the sacrifices. Who showed up, every single day.

Nalexia's phone rang.

Beckett's name flashed across the screen, and her car's Bluetooth picked up the call.

"Hey handsome!" she said, her voice trying to sound carefree.

“What’s up, my sweetbread,” Beckett said, voice smooth through the speakers. “I think I passed the parking garage. I’m turning around, but I’m close.”

Nalexia exhaled—tension pulsing behind her smile.

She wanted to believe him, but history whispered otherwise.

Late arrivals. Cancelled dates. Overbooked days. Beckett was a brilliant father, a business beast—but personal time? Always compromised.

Beckett could hear the guarded tone in her silence.

He understood. Their beginning was messy. Two kids, new responsibilities, expanding businesses. He went from solo dad of one to full-time father of *two*. He carried everything—and in the process, had failed to carry her.

He vowed tonight would be different.

Beckett finally pulled up beside her, stepped out of his car, and walked directly to her door.

He didn't rush.

He didn't make excuses.

He just took her hand.

Nalexia stepped out slowly. The way he looked at her made the cold air irrelevant. Her perfume—Razon, baby powder laced with soft musk—rose from her skin and stirred every part of him.

He kissed her, long and deep.

Then, hand in hand, they walked—one block over, another half block up—until they heard it. Music pulsing from the venue.

Beckett handed her an envelope. Inside: the tickets.

"You remembered," Nalexia smiled.

"I always do," Beckett replied.

Inside, the venue was dark and sensual. Black floors, black walls, and bodies pressed near a stage thick with anticipation and neon sweat. The air buzzed with sensuality—alcohol, smoke, and wild rhythms vibrating in sync with desire.

This was new for Nalexia. She'd been focused on school, motherhood, survival. A concert felt like a portal to a version of herself she forgot existed.

Across the room, she spotted familiar faces—Keolani and Yorick. Friends from back before everything shifted.

Keolani nudged her with a wink. "You made it!"

Beckett and Yorick exchanged their usual handshake-hug combo.

But then—Beckett's attention tunneled back to Nalexia. No distractions. Just her.

He walked to the bar, ordered their drinks, and had them sent over.

As the music picked up, Nalexia swayed with Keolani, drink in hand, body relaxed. It was rare to see her this loose, this open. She smiled—not for anyone else, but because *this* moment, *this* man… finally felt worth it.

She looked back at Beckett.

He was already watching her.

The band played. Ro Jame's erotic vocals wove into the haze of the smoke machine and the weed being passed behind the stage curtain. The lights bled violet and red and gold. Everyone danced like they were auditioning for someone's bedroom.

Nalexia turned to Beckett.

And pressed her hips into him.

It was subtle.

Then deliberate.

Her back to his chest, she rolled her body in time with the music. He slid his hands over her curves, his breath warming the shell of her ear. The room disappeared.

This was foreplay—public, unspoken, and thick with tension.

Beckett wanted her. Bad. But more than that, he wanted her to feel *wanted.* Valued. Seen. So he waited.

Three artists later, he leaned in.

"You ready to get out of here?" he asked, voice steady.

Nalexia turned, eyes searching his.

She saw everything—his desire, his restraint, his commitment.

"Yes," she breathed, soft but sure.

He didn't need to hear it over the music.

He just *knew*.

They slipped through the crowd, exiting into the night. Beckett walked closest to the street like he always did. The wind whipped between buildings, but neither of them cared.

They never noticed the man with the bulging eyes watching them from the shadows.

He wasn't there for love. He was there for leverage—anything that might help him charge Kimmy more.

As they approached their cars, Beckett's phone rang.

It was Doc.

Something had come up. He needed to leave. Bradley was about to be left alone.

Beckett's entire body stiffened. *Not tonight.*

But fatherhood didn't ask for permission.

He acted fast.

"Miss Kris," he said into the phone. "I know it's late, but can I ask you to stop by my place and stay with Bradley? I'll make it up to you."

Miss Kris had once run Charlotte's daycare. She was retired but still had a soft spot for Beckett and the kids.

After a pause, she agreed.

Next, he called Mitch. "Order a car for Miss Kris. Put it on my tab. Text me when she's arrived."

Problem solved. For now.

From her car, Nalexia watched Beckett pace, handling things like always. He didn't look panicked—but she knew what that meant. The moment was slipping away.

She debated leaving.

She didn't want to hear, *"I need to go."*

But something inside her whispered: *Stay. Trust him.*

By the time Beckett slipped back into his car, she was still there.

Still waiting.

Still believing.

Still hoping he would focus on her and the us they were trying to build.

Chapter 11

Nalexia's mind wandered. The memory of that dinner meeting with the new client replayed itself again—on loop. The potential deal was huge, but the moment had unraveled fast.

The builder the client was eager to introduce? Seth Stories.

Nalexia had heard from Kolanie that Seth was in town; she just never dreamed she would have to work with him.

As Seth walked toward the table, Nalexia's heart dropped—her glass of water slipping from her hand and shattering over the white linen.

Now, hours later replaying it all in her mind sitting in her car, her eyes glazed over, Nalexia was startled when Beckett tapped on the passenger window. She rolled down the window and forced a smile.

"You okay?" Beckett asked, concern etched into his face while he opened the passenger door and climbed in the car.

She rolled the driver's side window down, took a calming breath, and pushed past her instinct to shut down. "I'm okay. Just… got a lot on my mind."

Beckett didn't press. He knew better than to assume. "Do you want to talk about it?"

Instead of answering, Nalexia tapped her fingers on the steering wheel—debating. Before she could decide, Beckett reached for her hand. Then said, "whatever it is," his words were calm intentional and supportive, "we'll deal with it together. Tonight is about you. If you need to talk, I'm here. If you need to…" He winked. The wink made smile for the first time since he had gotten in the car. Still holding her hand they said together in silence comfortably. He waited. He had decided that he'd sit there with her all night if that's what she needed. The tenderness undid her. Nalexia burst into tears. Through a tight throat, the words tumbled out. "First, I was worried tonight's meeting would get cancelled. Then I had the meeting with the new client. The client is excited for me to manage his new property. He just had one caveat, I have to work with his builder to assure the project goes according to the original plans. He said he invited the builder to our table talk because the guy insisted on meeting me ahead of time. When the builder walked in—it was Seth."

She paused, watching Beckett closely. But he didn't flinch. He just held her hand, steady, letting her speak.

The silence made her stomach knot even tighter. Her shoulders shook as Beckett reached over and pulled her into his arms, cradling her across the center console. The position was uncomfortable, but he didn't care."It's okay," he whispered, rubbing her back.

And then it hit him.

Seth.

Choice's father?

Everything in Beckett wanted to pull away and demand answers—but Nalexia was already unraveling. This wasn't the time for ego. He forced his instincts down and focused on her instead.

After a few minutes, her breathing steadied.

Beckett asked softly, "So… he just walked in?"

Nalexia nodded, tears still glimmering in her eyes. "He acted like we were old lovers reunited. I held it together because I want this contract. I *need* this contract."

The truth grounded her again. "This deal would fulfill my obligations with the firm. It'll give me the freedom to finally go out on my own."

Beckett smiled with pride. "Sweetbread, you got this. If you have to work with your ex, then so be it. Let him see what he lost. You're a dynamic woman he can't have. You've outgrown the version of yourself that once loved him." His words didn't just comfort her—they *empowered* her.

He had watched her grind, study, raise her son, earn her BA, complete her broker training—*he knew her worth.*

Then he asked, "Why didn't you tell me sooner?"

Nalexia turned toward the wheel, then back to him. "Because… I didn't want you to feel the way I do when Kimmy does something unexpected."

Beckett understood immediately. That kind of tension was all too familiar.

He thought of all Nalexia had endured without complaint. Her quiet strength, her compassion—it moved him.

He kissed her.

Slowly.

Deeply.

Like a man who had finally found home. And in that kiss, Beckett knew—*she was the one*, like an additional confirmation confirming what he already knew.

"I've got an idea," he said, voice low. "Let's leave your car here. I'll have it brought to you later. I want to drive the rest of the night."

Nalexia smiled, curious and delighted. "What are you up to?"

"You'll see."

Beckett texted Mitch, he dropped a pen and instructed to pick up Nalexia's car and park it at her place. Mitch responded with a thumbs-up emoji.

"We're all set," Beckett said. "Let's roll."

They hit the road, heading out of Baltimore. The ride was light and full of laughter. They shared updates, inside jokes, memories only they would find funny. Nalexia didn't even realize they'd arrived until the car stopped.

Beckett parked in an empty lot outside a partially renovated building. Nalexia looked around.

"Honey… where are we?" Her voice danced between excitement and curiosity.

Beckett grinned. "This is your first building."

"What?"

He nodded, eyes glowing. "You're looking at the beginning of your real estate empire."

Inside the building, her sketches had come to life. Her dream of building a sustainable, tech-savvy community for single mothers—it was here.

Beckett had listened to every detail she'd ever shared and partnered with his engineering network to make it happen. Six more buildings would be finished in twelve weeks—just in time for her transition out of the firm.

Nalexia stood still, overwhelmed.

Room by room, they walked through the model apartment—four bedrooms, solar panels, built-in efficiency. Behind the main office sat the community center, with breakout rooms, a library, computer workstations, and a catering kitchen.

"I can't believe this," she whispered.

Memories of her first apartment returned. One-bedroom with a den. The den became Choice's nursery. Then came the eviction. The cold. The loss. The fish tank. Her laptop—*everything*—gone.

This was her redemption. And now, she could offer that hope to others.

"I want every tenant to go through debt counseling," she said, voice steady. "They deserve better than what I had."

Beckett's heart swelled. "I thought you might say that."

He handed her keys.

"Want to see what else I've got planned tonight?"

Ten minutes later, they pulled up to a modern office building.

“This will be your headquarters,” Beckett said. “Offices for leasing, nonprofit operations—and something special upstairs.”

They entered the building, and Beckett led her to the elevator. He used a key card to access the top floor marked with a *P*.

Inside the elevator, Nalexia wrapped her arms around him, burying her face in his chest. They inhaled each other—warm, breathless.

When the doors opened, Mitchell stood patiently waiting.

Nalexia jumped.

Beckett instinctively turned protectively until Mitchell grinned. “Hey boss. Hey Lex.”

He handed Beckett a device the size of a gaming console.

“Enjoy,” he said with a wink, stepping into the elevator and disappearing.

The penthouse suite was fully furnished. Soft lighting. Floor-to-ceiling windows. The city sparkled beyond the glass. Nalexia dropped her purse onto a chair.

“This is beautiful,” she whispered.

Beckett stepped away to check the security system.

When he turned, Nalexia was leaning against the wall—her romper and tights gone.

She wore only a black lace corset. Heels. And eyes full of heat.

He drew in a breath. She was art.

He stepped forward, his forearms resting on the wall above her head, his body pressing against hers.

Nalexia bit her lip as he teased his hands up and down her curves, every inch setting her on fire. He kissed her neck, let his breath dance over her skin before his lips did.

With gentle confidence, he lifted one leg, then the other—wrapping them around his shoulders.

The contrast between the cold wall behind her and the heat of his touch in front of her was electric.

She melted into him.

And he didn't stop until she unraveled completely—drenched in her own pleasure, her moans echoing into the ceiling.

Chapter 12

The entire time Beckett was exploring the depths of Nalexia's body, his phone had been buzzing relentlessly. The moment their passion slowed and reality crept back in, Nalexia reached into the tangle of their clothes and handed him his phone.

Thirty missed calls.

Beckett's heart dropped.

His security team had tried to reach him over and over. A man had been following Beckett and Nalexia. The team had detained him and contacted Beckett immediately—but with Mitchell gone and Beckett distracted, the calls had gone unanswered.

The phone lit up again.

Tyger.

Beckett's expression shifted. Tyger was the only person he would allow to interrupt this moment, because Tyger never called without reason—and if the kids were safe, this was about something else.

"What's good?" Beckett answered, his voice calm but alert.

Tyger's low, raspy voice came through. "I hate to break up your quality time, but duty calls. I need you to meet me now."

Beckett's jaw tightened. He looked over at Nalexia.

"Honey, get dressed. We have to go—now."

His tone told her everything.

Nalexia's chest tightened. Her thoughts immediately went to the children.

Beckett dressed quickly and led her out of the building. As they got into the car, he explained, "Tyger called about a potential security breach."

Nalexia exhaled in relief. The kids were fine—but a *security breach*? What did that mean?

The car sped through the city—Branch Avenue to Allentown Road, then onto Old Alexander Ferry. Beckett was quiet, focused. Nalexia didn't ask questions. She knew Beckett wouldn't let her ride along if he thought she was in danger. But the way he drove—tight-lipped, eyes like steel—told her this was serious.

They made a quick stop at a warehouse.

"Wait here," Beckett said, and disappeared inside.

Less than five minutes later, he was back. He didn't explain what he'd retrieved, and Nalexia didn't ask. She simply tightened her seatbelt. Whatever it was, she trusted him—and she knew he'd protect what mattered.

Tyger wasn't just Beckett's head of security—he was his childhood best friend, the one person who knew the full scope of Beckett's world.

After leaving private security and a few covert missions overseas, Tyger launched his own firm. His skills were unmatched—combat, tech, strategy—and his mind was always ten steps ahead. When Beckett's company, *Invention by Inventors*, began handling trade secrets and high-level deals, Tyger designed a legal trust to protect Beckett's identity as the owner.

People like Kimmy believed it was a scheme to dodge taxes or avoid paying more child support. The truth? It was bulletproof security.

Everything Beckett owned was in the business's name. His salary was traceable, taxable, and clean. But the empire was protected.

When Beckett and Nalexia arrived, Tyger was already mid-operation. The man who had been following them was being questioned in a rear office by Tyger's team. His name, according to the ID he provided, was *Mr. Brain.*

"He says Kimmy hired him," Tyger explained grimly. "She wanted someone to find out where you're hiding your money."

Beckett's jaw clenched.

Nalexia entered the room quietly—and gasped.

The man being interrogated looked roughed up. Blood dotted the corner of his mouth. Her eyes widened. Fear flickered across her face.

Tyger immediately noticed. He stepped in front of Beckett and lowered his voice so only Beckett could hear. “Maybe this is too much for her.”

Beckett turned to Nalexia. “You good heading out without me?”

Part of her didn’t want to leave—but she appreciated the out. This world… wasn’t hers. And she wasn’t ready to be pulled any deeper into its shadows.

Mitchell appeared, calm and reassuring. “Let’s get you home,” he said gently, leading her toward the exit.

Nalexia nodded. She wasn’t naïve. She knew there were things about Beckett’s life she hadn’t seen. But tonight made it clear—there was a line, and she wasn’t sure she was ready to cross it.

One of the security team drove her back to her condo.

Outside, as Beckett emerged from the building, Nalexia’s SUV was pulling away. Tyger followed close behind.

To an outsider, the whole scene looked like business as usual.

Tyger chuckled. "So Kimmy had the balls to hire someone to track your money? That's wild."

Beckett's expression was flat. "She's not dumb. She just thinks everybody owes her something."

Tyger grinned, but there was tension behind it. "Remember when we started this thing? We were just trying to make fifty grand a year. Now? The company's booming. You've got contracts coming in like wildfire, and Kimmy's been watching too close for comfort."

He wasn't wrong. Beckett's company paid employees well, poured back into the community, and had an expense account that most executives would envy. Kimmy didn't want accountability—she wanted a piece of the empire.

Beckett stayed silent, then looked toward the warehouse.

Inside, Mr. Brain had finished talking. He'd confirmed Kimmy hired him to dig into Beckett's finances. The job was dirty, but it gave them what they needed.

Beckett exhaled. "Let him go. He told us what we needed."

Tyger turned, relaying the order to the team.

"You heard him. Turn him loose!"

Some of the newer hires hesitated, looking to Tyger for confirmation.

Tyger shook his head. "I swear, these new guys don't get it. Beckett says move—you move."

Truth was, Tyger had anticipated this. He'd already implanted a micro-tracker in Mr. Brain's neck. Letting him go meant he'd lead them right back to Kimmy—or anyone else on her payroll.

It was better this way. Kimmy needed to be dealt with directly, not through pawns.

Mitchell, meanwhile, had returned to the warehouse to oversee operations. The security team resumed their assignments.

The war wasn't over.

But tonight, a line had been drawn.

And Beckett was ready to defend it.

Chapter 13

Sunday morning broke with a knock at the door.

Beckett, still shirtless, crossed the condo with deliberate calm. As he moved through the living space, he paused to appreciate the design touches—Nalexia's favorite soft tones infused with his sleek modern taste, masterfully blended into every corner of the penthouse. The home wasn't just a place—it was *them*.

His phone buzzed relentlessly on the couch, vibrating like it was having a meltdown. He ignored it.

Unbothered, Beckett unlocked the elevator and the front door. Mitchell pushed inside in a panic, words tumbling out before the door even shut behind him.

"Boss, we got a problem—a *real* one. We're in danger. Things need to be fixed, *now*."

Beckett didn't flinch. He rarely did. Calm was his default. But the tension behind Mitchell's eyes registered.

From the hallway, Nalexia appeared, barefoot in a short, pink satin robe. Her hair was still tousled from the night. She blinked, surprised at the commotion.

Beckett's phone buzzed again.

Nalexia glanced at him, giving that silent *breathe and ground him* look—the one she gave when she needed him not just present, but composed. He caught the signal and nodded, shifting gears.

Meanwhile, Nalexia stepped into the kitchen, drawn to the gleaming waterfall island and the stocked cabinets. She hadn't fully explored the space yet—not after Beckett made good on his promise to love her in every room. The idea of a slow morning was gone now, replaced with adrenaline and ringing phones.

She brewed a pot of coffee, then made herself a dirty chai tea using the espresso machine. In the background, Mitchell's voice shifted from frantic to focused.

"Tyger's been trying to reach you," he said, more composed now.

Beckett finally picked up his phone and played a voicemail.

“Ay—it’s been a breach at the warehouse. Alarms are going off like crazy. I need you to meet me.” —Tyger

Beckett’s jaw tightened. He turned to Nalexia.

“Get dressed, baby.”

Then softer, following her toward the bedroom: “Where’s your laptop? I want to review the system data before we get to the site.”

From the living room, Mitchell answered for her. “Boss, I grabbed your tablet and her laptop—left them on the mail table by the door.”

When Beckett returned dressed in sweats and sneakers, he was already on the phone with Tyger, holding it to his ear, not on speaker. Nalexia, now dressed in jeans and a fitted sweater, raised an eyebrow.

“Wait—offsite building? What’s going on?”

Beckett kissed her forehead. “I’ll explain everything. But you’re coming with me.”

He’d considered leaving her behind—safe, untouched by this mess—but after everything they'd faced together, leaving her in the dark now didn't feel right.

Tyger met them at the offsite location, already in full operations mode.

"Okay," Tyger began, "the Mr. Brain character has an accomplice. I figured it out after our last talk. This breach? It could be them, or a rival company responding to that two million from the event. Either way, I've got my team digging."

Nalexia spoke up. "Should I be worried? For myself? For the kids?"

Her eyes darted between Beckett and Tyger, reading the unspoken tension in their body language.

There was a beat of silence.

Mitchell—hoping to ease the air—spoke out of turn. "Once Beckett talks to Kimmy, this'll all clear up."

Nalexia's entire posture shifted. Grace gone. Kindness paused.

"What is *that bitch's* problem?! Why can't she just move the *fuck* on?!"

She stormed down the hallway. She was done with the drama—*over it.* She had her own life, her own business to run. She didn't have time for childish vendettas.

Inside the bedroom, she quickly changed into a sexy but professional outfit, spraying perfume before grabbing her Tory Burch work bag. Her keys clinked in her hand as she returned to the living room, collected but emotionally spent.

Beckett said nothing. But he felt it.

The weight of Kimmy's drama was slowly corroding something sacred.

Meanwhile, Tyger's trusted security team began pouring into the condo, setting up for digital forensics and sweeping for vulnerabilities. Nalexia felt suffocated. The space—once luxurious—suddenly felt like a cage. She passed through the condo like a ghost, brushing past strangers in her home, the walls seemingly closing in.

Beckett had security pick up the children—Bradley, Charlotte, and Choice—and bring them to the condo. Doc helped get them settled. Bradley read quietly, Charlotte napped, and Choice gamed near the couch.

Mitchell brought a computer engineer to work alongside Tyger's team. They uncovered something sickening.

Low-budget investigators had accessed Beckett and Nalexia's *devices*. They had recordings—of them making love. Video. Audio.

Beckett stood frozen. This wasn't just a security breach. It was a violation.

He'd feared his past might endanger Nalexia or the kids. But now it wasn't just a fear—it was real.

In the kitchen, Nalexia was quiet. Too quiet. Her chill was colder than silence.

Beckett approached gently. "Please, be careful," he said.

"I heard you," she replied. Her voice was firm, emotion buried beneath steel.

She kissed the children goodbye, clutched her purse, and walked to the elevator. Beckett caught her expression just before the doors closed—a look he'd never seen from her before.

He didn't need words to understand:

Fix this. Or *lose her*.

Back inside, Tyger and Mitchell followed Beckett into the soundproof study, closing the sliding doors. Beckett dropped into his desk chair, hands locked in thought. No words. Just the slow burn of everything unraveling.

Tyger paced on the phone. Mitchell waited silently.

Beckett replayed all the ways Nalexia had stood by him—loved him for who he was, not what he gave her. She didn't need the lifestyle. She worked hard. She had a plan. And she *chose* him.

His voice finally returned. "I need to know everything those investigators found—and what they could've shared with Kimmy."

Tyger was already uploading evidence to Beckett's tablet. Mitchell summoned a few more staff into the room. One by one, tablets, timelines, audio logs, surveillance images—everything came flooding in.

It went as far back as the hotel surprise Beckett had orchestrated for Nalexia.

As Beckett reviewed the data, his heart grew heavier. The recordings. The breach. The betrayal.

He didn't flinch until Tyger said:

"Young—you *need* to hear this."

Tyger played the clip.

It was the audio recording. Of *that* night.

Beckett's calm shattered. "What *else* did they find?!"

His voice boomed through the study's walls. Even the kids paused mid-play, instinctively sensing his rage.

Tyger and Mitchell stood in place as Beckett paced like a storm preparing to make landfall.

Later, outside the study, Tyger pulled Beckett aside in the hallway.

"You want me to handle this?" he asked quietly.

Beckett gave a short, direct: "Yes. But wait for my call."

Tyger nodded. But before walking away, he added, "Bec—some guy named Seth emailed Nalexia. His name's familiar. You want me to keep an eye on him?"

Beckett paused.

From the corner, Mitchell's head snapped toward them. He'd seen the email too. Seth wasn't just anyone. He was *Seth Stories*—and he was *Choice's* father.

Beckett exhaled.

"Not yet," he said. "Let that one breathe."

But inside, he was already calculating.

The war was coming from all sides.

And if he didn't win—he wouldn't just lose control.

He'd lose *her*.

Chapter 14

Nalexia leaned over Beckett's caramel-tan desk, locking eyes with him, unflinching. The tension between them filled the air like smoke in a closed room. From the doorway, Mitchell froze, sensing the weight of the moment.

"Boss—" he started.

Beckett didn't even blink. "*Not now*."

Nalexia didn't move. Didn't flinch. Her brow was raised, lips pursed, her perfectly manicured fingers spread and planted firmly on the desk like she was anchoring her emotions. It wasn't just a stare—it was a *stance*. A silent message:

You're not going to control me.

Beckett respected her fire. Loved it. Needed it. But this wasn't just a stare-down—it was a war between fear and trust, protection and independence. He hated the idea of her going to dinner with Seth alone, and she knew it.

From outside the office, the clanging of tools and yelling from the warehouse crew rose, then faded. Mitchell's voice came again, sharper this time. "Boss! Your ex-wife is here."

And just like that, Nalexia had leverage.

She smirked. That single brow still arched. Then she stood straight, calmly smoothing her fitted black skirt. Her sculpted legs moved with intentional grace as she walked past Mitchell and straight out of the office.

She didn't flinch as she passed Kimmy—Beckett's *first wife*. In fact, the look she gave her was equal parts disdain and amusement, like a queen watching a jester try to storm her court.

The warehouse was chaos: drills buzzing, metal clanging, voices shouting. Beckett was already on edge from the deadline—and Nalexia knew that. She *liked* when he was on edge. It made him primal. Possessive. But it also meant he'd need her closer.

She was willing to be that place of peace.

But only if he loved her with excellence.

Beckett exited through the side door, blinking into the sunlight just in time to catch the sight of Nalexia heading toward her car. The way her blouse hugged her, the wind catching her long, loose curls—it stopped his breath. Kimmy stood nearby, watching. But Beckett only saw *her*.

He caught up and gently reached for her hand, pressing a kiss to each of her fingers before speaking.

"You are one of the most important people in my life," he said quietly. "And I hate the thought of you having dinner with Seth."

Nalexia didn't answer. Just lifted her chin slightly, eyes cool.

"I need you to push the dinner back. Eight p.m. That's the only way I'll be okay with it."

Still, she said nothing. Instead, she tilted her head toward the warehouse.

"We have an audience."

Beckett looked into her eyes, closer now. "You are mine. *All* mine. I will *not* have you out unprotected. I don't trust Seth."

But Nalexia's response was clipped, her tone cold. "You need to deal with *that mess*."

Beckett didn't argue. He pulled her into him, holding her close. There was pain in her voice, and he knew why—this was the first time her *past* was affecting their *present*.

His voice dropped, full of power and promise. "*You. Are. The. Only. Person. Who. Matters.*"

Each word was slow. Intentional. A beat that pierced through her defenses.

Nalexia softened. Her shoulders lowered. Her breath caught. Then, Beckett kissed her.

Their lips parted together, and tension turned into something else—heat, longing, connection. The ground beneath them seemed to shift.

But just as the moment deepened, Mitchell burst through the door.

"Boss! We got a *problem*."

Beckett exhaled in frustration. He didn't want to let her go—but he also couldn't lose control of the situation brewing inside. Carefully, he opened the car door and watched his queen drive off before turning to face the fire.

Kimmy was still standing there, stone-faced and silent.

Beckett walked right past her. "What do you need?"

Kimmy wanted to scream. Curse. Throw something. But instead, she played it cool, bluffing with courtroom threats.

"Tyger said you wanted to talk," she snapped.

He didn't slow down. "I do. But not *now*."

Kimmy clenched her jaw. He had never looked at *her* the way he looked at Nalexia. Never kissed her fingers. Never said words like *you matter*.

Inside the warehouse, alarms blared. Chaos erupted. Fire extinguishers were being passed around. Workers scrambled.

Beckett finally turned, facing her with steady eyes.

"What do you expect from me?"

The question hit her like a slap. Before she could answer, Mitchell's voice called from deep in the building.

Without looking back, Beckett said, "I need to handle this. See yourself out."

He was gone. Just like that.

And all eyes turned to Kimmy.

She stood frozen for a beat, throat tight with shame and fury. Her chest rose and fell as tears rushed to the surface. She turned and stormed toward the exit. Her sister's words haunted her:

"Maybe you should try getting to know him instead of trying to trap him into taking care of you."

By the time Kimmy reached the door, she was running—half from grief, half from rage.

She didn't see the car parked down the street.

Didn't know that someone was watching her.

Chapter 15

Nalexia was still simmering from her last encounter with Beckett, but she picked up her phone anyway and called Seth. Beckett had insisted on being present at dinner—said it was the perfect time for him to formally meet the man who'd be running point on the contract. Seth had apparently proven himself to the business owner, and that meant Nalexia would be working directly with him for the rest of the deal.

That was what pushed Beckett to rearrange his entire schedule.

Seth answered on the first ring, his voice warm and familiar. Too familiar. "Hey, you—just the person I needed to talk to."

Nalexia didn't engage his tone. "I think it's best we move the dinner to 8 p.m."

Seth had originally invited her to meet him at 10 p.m. at the lounge in his hotel. Nalexia hadn't even accepted the invite. She had called his office instead and redirected the meeting to a restaurant near her firm. She needed the boundary.

To her surprise, Seth didn't push back. "Eight works for me. It's a date. I can't wait to see you."

His voice oozed nostalgia, and Nalexia's stomach flipped. It wasn't excitement. It was *dread*.

Seth was still reckless—blatantly ignoring the fact that Beckett would be joining them. The whole thing felt off. Nalexia had only agreed to meet over dinner instead of at the firm because, in truth, she wanted Beckett to understand what it felt like for the *past* to disrupt the *present*. She needed him to know that her love wasn't just convenient—it was a daily choice. A costly one.

She thought about everything she'd endured—how Melissa and Kimmy had both dragged Beckett through emotional chaos, and how she'd stayed. Supported him. She thought of their friendship, their bond, their unmatched communication. But the call with Seth reminded her just how fragile it all could be.

More than anything, it reminded her:

She only wanted Beckett.

But she also needed to talk to him about how deeply his people-pleasing tendencies—especially with Melissa and Kimmy—were starting to weigh on her.

Her phone rang again.

“Did you forget about me?” Elle’s Boston accent came through thick.

“I could never forget you,” Nalexia said, relieved to hear a friendly voice. “I’ve just been grinding—trying to close out these last few contracts.”

Elle lowered her voice, likely at the office. “Girl, I *heard.* I’m so proud of you. But wait… is it *true*? Is Seth really the rep?”

Nalexia groaned. “Ugh. Yes.”

Elle gasped like the drama just got juicy. Nalexia chuckled and said, “Let me jump off—I’m pulling up to my next appointment.”

“Fine, but I want *details* later.”

Nalexia hung up and grabbed her purse. She was meeting Keolani for their long-delayed nail appointment—something they’d planned since before the concert night.

She parked beside Keolani's red Dodge Charger and headed into the salon. As soon as she stepped inside, Tyler—the owner—grinned.

"How's my favorite billionaire-in-the-making?"

Nalexia smiled. Everyone loved Beckett. Especially in neighborhoods he'd grown up in and now reinvested in.

Tyler was a true fan. Beckett had one of his inventors test the "mood room" concept in Tyler's salon, and it blew up on TikTok. Spa parties were now booked months in advance.

"How's life?" Nalexia greeted Tyler as she sat next to Keolani at the nail station.

Tyler flared with flair. "Life's *grand*! I can't keep these bougie heifers outta that room Bec built me. And just last week, Tyger installed a sound system *and* a fragrance thingy!"

"Fragrance thingy?" Keolani raised a brow.

"Yeah! That little box releases a scent just for this space. Tyger says Neiman Marcus and that purple mattress store use stuff like this."

They laughed as Tyler placed bowls of warm water in front of them. Keolani leaned toward Nalexia, shifting the tone.

"So… how are *you*?"

Nalexia sighed and went straight to it. "I'm good. I'd be better if my *ex* wasn't the point man on my final contract."

Tyler and Keolani screamed in unison.

"Your *final* contract?!" Tyler repeated. "That's major!"

Nalexia nodded. "After this, I'm out. No more firm obligations."

Tyler's voice dropped. "Wait… *Choice's* father? That ex?"

Startled, Nalexia jerked her hand and almost knocked over the water bowl. They managed to save it, but grabbed towels to clean the splash.

Tyler's station sat on a raised platform in the salon for his VIP clients, offering some privacy, even as the rest of the shop buzzed.

Keolani, still calm, gave herself away.

"*You knew!*" Tyler accused.

Keolani winced. "He called me about a month ago. Said he was trying to get hired at Tolerverb."

"They're that tech company moving to the DMV from Cali, right?"

"Exactly."

They all exchanged looks. Beckett wouldn't like this. Especially with Seth sniffing around again.

Tyler huffed, then softened. "Okay, enough about Seth. How are the babies?"

Keolani added, "Still in practice mode for when we *maybe* need a baby shower one day." She winked.

They all laughed. Nalexia relaxed enough to pick her nail color.

"Oh—the kids are great. They act like they've been siblings forever. Beckett had to bring them to the condo after Kimmy popped up at the warehouse *again*."

Keolani slammed her hand on the table.

"Ugh! I wanna beat that girl one good time. Just drag her."

Tyler grabbed nearby bottles before they fell. The mood lightened as they shifted to talking about Tyler's wild love life and TikTok drama.

Once their nails were done and dry, they all parted ways. But as Nalexia walked to her car, her thoughts returned to Seth, Beckett, and that dinner.

She didn't know what the night would bring.

But she knew this much—whatever happened, her heart wasn't up for grabs. It already belonged to Beckett.

Chapter 16

Back in her car, Nalexia dialed Beckett.

"Hey, Sweetbread," she said. "How's Tyler enjoying the upgrade Tyger installed?"

Beckett sounded winded, like he'd sprinted to get to the phone. But before he could answer, Nalexia jumped ahead.

"Honey, I'm worried about this meeting with Seth."

Her words made Beckett pause. He could hear the tension in her voice. His tone dropped into something slower, more grounded.

"What's the worst thing Seth could tell me about you?"

Nalexia blinked, surprised by the question.

Beckett continued before she could speak. "I know how most relationships start—chemistry, sex, routine. So, what's the worst he could say?"

Nalexia went quiet. Then her voice softened. "When I was with Seth… he made me feel like he was the only stable thing in my world. I'd try to move on, date other guys, but every time one of them disappointed me, Seth would reappear. He always knew the perfect moment to pop back in. He was the first man I really shared myself with."

She hated admitting it out loud, hated how much of herself she'd given to someone so manipulative. But she needed Beckett to hear it from her—not from Seth.

Beckett sat with her honesty, letting it settle. He loved her fiercely, and that meant loving all of her—even the parts she wished she could erase.

"So," he asked gently, "do you think this is one of those times? Me doing something stupid… and Seth swooping back in?"

The question hit Nalexia harder than expected. "No," she said quickly. "Not at all. I'm happy in our relationship."

The rhythmic click of her turn signal filled the silence.

"Yes, we've got things to work on—but that's just life. I just… I need you to know that Seth was like a boomerang maintenance man. He'd show up right when I was fixing things."

Beckett hated picturing her with another man—but he respected her more for being honest. Her transparency made him love her deeper, not less.

Nalexia felt a pang of fear—had she said too much? But she pushed through it. There couldn't be blind spots between them, especially not where Seth was concerned.

Mitchell knocked on the office door, stepping in. Beckett glanced at the time.

"Honey, I've gotta go. But I'll call you once I'm en route."

Beckett still hadn't dealt with Kimmy, but it was time. She'd been waiting for hours before Mitchell finally led her back to the office.

Kimmy entered and immediately closed the door behind her.

Beckett had already briefed Mitchell: *Never leave me completely alone with her.*

Moments later, Mitchell returned, knocking once before stepping back in.

"Boss—they're ready for the test. If I prop the door open, you can see everything from your desk."

Beckett nodded, appreciating the cover. Mitchell was more than a loyal employee—he would've taken a bullet for Beckett if life ever demanded it.

"You don't mind if we leave the door open?" Beckett asked Kimmy, already gesturing toward it.

She rolled her eyes and shifted in her chair. "Do whatever you need to do."

Kimmy didn't recognize anyone in Beckett's world. She walked in with a "hate the world" attitude, and it filled the room.

Beckett's tone turned cool. Almost icy.

"You've been showing up a lot lately. What is it you want now?"

Kimmy hated how cold he'd become. She wasn't a woman he loved anymore—just a liability he managed.

She tried summoning tears. Nothing came.

"I want to go back to mediation."

Beckett raised his eyebrows, stunned. *Of all things…*

"Why?"

He didn't want to guide her answers. Just let her speak and watch what she revealed.

"I need a break," Kimmy sighed. "Charlotte needs so much. Parenting alone is hard."

The audacity made Beckett's stomach turn. He thought back to how Kimmy had originally lost full custody due to neglect. How she later manipulated a panel of professionals to regain shared custody, claiming no child should be separated from their mother.

He remembered the entire ugly truth.

Kimmy had never wanted intimacy. She'd treated sex like a dirty obligation—until one night when, out of the blue, she seduced him. It felt forced. Mechanical. Unnatural.

What Beckett didn't know then was that she had spent that week taking fertility supplements. That night, after they were done, she had locked herself in the bathroom and done a *headstand*—trying to trap him into fatherhood.

Three months later, Kimmy sat across from him with trembling lips and whispered, “I’m pregnant.”

Beckett had already planned to end the relationship. But instead, he buried his needs and did what he thought a man was supposed to do—step up and prepare to be a father again.

They married. Slept in separate rooms. Faked happiness for outsiders.

Eleven months of misery.

And now she was here, smug in his office, asking for a *break.*

“What exactly do you have in mind?” Beckett asked.

He was already covering all of Charlotte’s needs—financial, emotional, logistical. He’d missed date nights with Nalexia. Skipped family outings. Rearranged his entire schedule. And Kimmy still wanted more.

She leaned across the desk, trying to mimic what Nalexia had done just hours earlier. But where Nalexia radiated grace and conviction, Kimmy reeked of manipulation.

Beckett pushed his wheeled chair back, creating space.

"I'll gladly take more quality time with my daughter," he said plainly.

Kimmy didn't realize that statement was a trap—one she'd walked into willingly. Beckett was three moves ahead, even on his worst days.

Kimmy thought she'd won. She had no idea that Beckett had planned their divorce so meticulously that her lawyers only ever saw him earning $50,000 a year. He had hidden his wealth. Hidden his holdings. Hidden his true power.

She assumed he was just a "mid-grade hustler" scared of words like *court*, *custody*, and *child support*.

She was wrong.

Kimmy left his office feeling victorious. The warehouse clanged and buzzed with machine noise. She didn't hear Mitchell mutter under his breath as she passed, "*Triflin'*..."

"Boss, you good?" Mitchell reentered, genuine concern in his eyes.

Beckett nodded, then motioned him in.

"Sit for a minute."

He spoke slowly, deliberately.

"If you don't express love clearly, consistently… the people who matter most won't know how much they matter. We can't afford to be unclear with the ones we care about."

Mitchell soaked it in. He always did. He saw Beckett as more than a boss. Beckett was the man who gave him a real shot at life.

After a few moments, Beckett glanced at the time.

Time to shift gears.

He briefed Mitchell on the remaining deadlines and prepped him to lead the next day's operations. Beckett believed in Mitchell's potential—even if Mitchell hadn't fully seen it yet.

Then Beckett grabbed his keys and headed to his midnight blue Infiniti.

He started the car and drove off the warehouse property.

It was time to face the night—and Seth.

Chapter 17

Nalexia was in the shower when her Bluetooth speaker cut out mid–Brittany Spears anthem.

“Call incoming,” the device announced.

Assuming it was Beckett calling to say he was on his way, Nalexia tapped “Answer.”

“Hey, handsome, where are you?” she said playfully, voice echoing against the steamed-up tiles.

Outside the bathroom, Beckett had already let himself in. He’d heard her voice from the hall—and now stood frozen in the doorway, confused. She thought *he* was on the phone?

Then a male voice responded.

“Hey, you!” The tone was too casual, too familiar. Beckett paused, lips tightening.

Nalexia immediately froze. That voice. She knew it too well.

“Who is this?” she snapped, shutting off the water.

The mirror was fogged over. Even though the caller couldn't see her, she instinctively wrapped her arms around her body.

"Aww, I'm offended. You don't know my voice anymore?" he teased, laughing.

"Seth," she muttered under her breath, disgust rising in her chest.

"It's me, sexy little thang." His words dripped with that same arrogance that used to charm her. But now? It turned her stomach.

"What do you want, Seth?" Her tone dropped like a steel door.

He chuckled, unfazed. "Just wanted to make sure you got the address change for our meeting."

"I told you to coordinate through the office," she said tightly, grabbing a towel. But she caught herself—she couldn't afford to seem difficult right now. "Anyway, I'm sure Beckett and I can find it. See you there."

Before he could respond, she hung up.

Across the room, Beckett was still standing on the other side of the bathroom door, jaw clenched. He knew everyone had a past—but *this* was a man who thought he still had access.

The door opened.

Beckett quickly took a seat on the bedroom loveseat, pretending to scroll through documents on his tablet.

Nalexia walked in, towel-clad and distracted. She sat at her vanity, grabbed her Razac lotion, and began rubbing it into her skin—slow, pensive strokes as her thoughts raced.

Finally, she spoke.

"Seth called while I was in the shower."

Her voice was small. Nervous. Like a child admitting something wrong.

"I don't know how he got my number," she continued. "I told him to use the office, but he said he was just confirming the location. I texted you the new address."

Beckett kept his head down.

"I just… I felt weird," Nalexia added. "Like answering the phone was a betrayal. I didn't want you to—"

"I heard you," Beckett said quietly.

Nalexia blinked. "What?"

"I heard you," he repeated, louder now.

She stood, lotion in hand, unsure of what to do next.

"I heard you on the phone," Beckett said again. "And I don't want to imagine you with another man. But I can't be mad about what came before me. We all have a past."

He stood, walked over, and gently slid his hands into her damp hair.

Then he kissed her.

It was deep. Slow. Possessive. His lips poured reassurance into her soul.

Nalexia melted into him, craving more. Craving *all* of him.

She dropped her towel.

Without a word, her hands lifted to her full breasts, coaxing desire into the space between them. Beckett groaned low in his throat. He didn't care if they were late now.

Jamie Foxx's "Do What It Do" came through the Bluetooth speaker just as they stumbled into the bathroom. Beckett's phrase for these moments was *Love Session*—a sacred ritual where he loved Nalexia's body until she erupted three times.

He knew every curve, every sigh. Her bitten lip. Her trembling leg. The way she whispered his name like a prayer.

And when it was over, Beckett gently poured Dove's coconut body wash into his hands and washed every inch of her. Then she washed him, their movements unhurried, their intimacy electric.

Eventually, Beckett forced himself out of the bathroom to get dressed. He walked into the closet where his wardrobe was arranged by color, season, and style. He selected a sleek, dark outfit and stepped into it with ease.

At her vanity, Nalexia pinned her thick, wavy hair into a soft updo. By the time they were dressed, there was a knock at the door.

Mitchell.

He stepped inside with a nod—always calm, always put together. His loyalty was evident in every move.

Mitchell handed Beckett a packet of documents, and the two exchanged a brief but meaningful handshake.

Mitchell left.

Beckett helped Nalexia into her jacket before grabbing her bag and heading out.

Outside, Beckett opened the door of his freshly delivered iridium blue Infiniti Q60. As Nalexia slid in, he took one long look at her legs.

Focus, he told himself.

He drove with the windows down, letting the warm night air glide across Nalexia's skin. Raheem DeVaughn's smooth vocals spilled from the speakers. Beckett rested his hand on her thigh, grounding her, claiming her.

Seth had sent the new meeting location: the Residence Inn at National Harbor. Nalexia hadn't commented—she just forwarded the message.

When they pulled up, she looked anxious.

"Babe," Beckett said gently, "he can't divide us. There's nothing he can say."

Nalexia squeezed his hand.

Inside the lobby, they spotted Seth already seated. Nalexia introduced them quickly, placing her bag beside her.

Beckett pulled out her chair and watched Seth closely.

Seth hesitated but took a seat.

No words were needed—Beckett's presence spoke for itself. Confident. Commanding.

"Did you receive the documents I sent?" Nalexia asked.

Seth fumbled with his phone. "Uhh…"

"No worries," she said smoothly, forwarding the email again. Then she angled her tablet toward both men and launched into her presentation.

“This project is a game-changer. Once we break ground, we’ll attract the next round of investors. I’ve structured it in phases to increase long-term yield.”

Beckett nodded, following her logic. He already knew the details—but admired how Nalexia worked the room.

“Seth,” Beckett said suddenly, “are you lead architect for all phases or just phase one?”

“Phase one?” Seth asked, confused.

Beckett already knew the answer.

The questions continued. Seth fumbled. Sweated. Backpedaled.

It became clear he hadn’t reviewed the full proposal—and likely hadn’t even *received* the initial version.

Before Nalexia could smooth things over, Seth called his boss.

Moments later, a video call was live. Nalexia introduced Beckett and recapped the value of her phased approach. Her voice was confident. Clear.

By the end of the call, everything was signed. The deal was done.

Seth's boss asked Beckett for his number before ending the meeting.

Beckett's phone rang immediately after.

He kissed the back of Nalexia's hand and stepped away to answer.

Seth took his shot.

He reached across the table and brushed Nalexia's hand.

She jerked back like he'd burned her.

"Ahh, don't be like that," he said with a smirk. "You know you're the one that got away. Seeing you talk business like that… it's a whole new you. When did you learn all this stuff?"

The question made Nalexia blink.

I was in school when we met, she wanted to say. *You just never cared to notice.*

For the first time, she truly saw him.

Desperate.

Unprepared.

Petty.

The truth clicked into place: Seth hadn't read the documents because he wasn't even CC'd. He only drew up the original plans because he *needed* the money—cutting himself out of future phases, forfeiting royalties, and operating without vision.

She glanced at Beckett—then back at Seth.

The comparison wasn't even close.

"Sweetbread, you ready?" Beckett called.

Perfect timing.

"Yes," Nalexia said, rising. "I'm ready."

Seth stood awkwardly as they left.

"Great meeting!" he called out behind them—his voice more uncertain than enthusiastic.

Nalexia didn't look back. But something inside her shifted.

She wasn't afraid anymore.

She was free.

Chapter 18

The next morning, Beckett's phone rang. It was Gee Forstmon—Seth's boss.

"Mr. Beckett," Gee said warmly, "I'll be in town for a few days. I'd love to meet you in person."

As Beckett was wrapping up the call, Nalexia walked into the kitchen, barefoot and focused. "Honey, the owner of my firm just contacted me," she said, grabbing a glass of water. "Apparently, I'm required to attend a dinner meeting with Gee Forstmon tonight. They said my contract exit agreement depends on it."

Beckett bristled. He despised how the firm used Nalexia—pushing her brilliance forward while offering no support. "Let me help," he said, slipping his phone back in his pocket. "Gee just called me too. Let me take the reins on this. I'll text him now and set everything up so you can walk in and shine."

Nalexia exhaled. She had thought securing the signed development contract was enough. But her firm wanted more—they wanted the dinner to go *perfectly*. And they were making her prove herself again.

Beckett could see the strain in her eyes. And he wouldn't let her face it alone.

He made a few calls, and by early afternoon, everything was locked in. A private venue. Curated guest list. Controlled environment. His team was in motion.

Meanwhile, Nalexia sharpened her PowerPoint, revising her projections and preparing answers for every potential objection. Beckett had the kids spend a few extra days with Doc, who loved their company. With the house quiet, they could both focus.

That evening, Nalexia was ready.

They arrived at a cozy, upscale Peruvian restaurant just after dusk. Beckett parked and came around to open Nalexia's door, reaching out his hand to help her step onto the cobblestone curb. She smiled. He was always so attentive, so present. She felt wrapped in safety and admiration.

As they walked hand-in-hand toward the entrance, a member of the wait staff held the door open with a courteous nod. Nalexia noticed a sign near the entry:

"Closed to the Public – Private Event."

She blinked in surprise. *Had Beckett rented out the entire restaurant?*

He had.

Beckett knew that a win tonight would do more than help her career—it would help her believe again. In herself. In what was possible.

Earlier that morning, Gee had casually mentioned that his girlfriend—a high-profile public figure—would be accompanying him. Beckett took that information and acted. Tyger's security team handled everything: airport pickup, transport, on-site surveillance. Inside and outside, the restaurant was secured.

The restaurant owner came over personally. "Mr. Becks, thank you for covering our tax bill. You saved our family restaurant. The upgrades you funded made this place look brand new. And Mr. Tyger's work on our website and social media? Incredible. Twenty food bloggers coming next week for our grand opening—we're beyond grateful."

He introduced his son, then stepped away. A musician appeared from the back, playing soft Peruvian melodies on a charango, setting the mood.

Gee and his girlfriend arrived first. They greeted Beckett and Nalexia like old friends, not business associates. Laughter and warmth filled the room.

Seth arrived next—with a date.

Nalexia's stomach dropped slightly.

The woman on Seth's arm was Kimmy.

Last to arrive was the firm's representative. Once the full party was assembled, the restaurant owner's son led them to a newly renovated banquet room in the back.

Nine large flatscreens lined one wall, looping Nalexia's sleek PowerPoint presentation with crisp transitions and high-end renderings. The table was set with a chef-curated tasting menu, paired with wine.

Gee smiled. "Let's eat first. Get to know each other. Then we'll talk business."

Everyone took their seats.

Nalexia was stunned to see Kimmy sitting across the table—but she didn't flinch. Not tonight.

Beckett's presence anchored her. His wit kept the table laughing, and when Nalexia shared a funny story from her week, even Gee's girlfriend leaned in to listen.

Gee opened up about stepping into his father's company and his desire to make this project a signature move—something bold enough to separate him from his family legacy.

Beckett nodded in empathy.

Seth and Kimmy remained mostly quiet, their energy noticeably different from the rest of the group.

After dinner, the presentation began.

Nalexia guided the room through each slide with poise. Beckett and Gee were especially impressed with how she used AI to reconfigure Seth's original plans, doubling the projected tenant count while maintaining structural and aesthetic integrity.

"This new phase of residential units," Nalexia explained, "creates opportunities for displaced families—particularly those coming from subsidized housing as a result of the sale."

She glanced at the firm rep, who lifted a glass in clear approval.

Gee's girlfriend leaned in. "How many total units?"

"Excellent question," Nalexia replied. "Each corner of the building will house a luxury unit—two levels, upstairs and down. In total, there will be 1,000 residential units. Our firm will retain ownership of 200, including 50 subsidized units. The rest will be evenly split between Gee and his investors."

Kimmy suddenly raised a hand.

"What about security?" Her tone was clipped, her posture tense. "This area isn't exactly prime real estate. Tenants like *her*"—she gestured at Gee's girlfriend—"won't feel safe living here."

The room fell still.

Nalexia stood. Her voice was calm, but steel-lined. "Actually, when my firm acquired this property, the city required a revitalization plan. Our intention is to restore—not relocate—the community."

She clicked to the next slide.

"This," she said, pointing to the screen, "is one of Beckett's affiliate companies. They'll handle on-site security and community patrols, working alongside local law enforcement."

Gee's girlfriend perked up. "Oh, *that* team? They escorted us from the airport. Impeccable service. I already called my agency to add them to our permanent roster."

Nalexia beamed.

On the next slide, she presented the confirmed business tenants: a childcare provider, barber/salon, gym with therapy and nutrition services, and other essential lifestyle vendors.

Kimmy scoffed. "Therapy? You're trippin'. People from this area can't afford that."

Seth finally spoke.

He squeezed Kimmy's hand gently. "Actually, that's not true. Nalexia structured the leases so those services are bundled into tenant agreements. Residents receive access automatically. It's… genius."

He looked at Nalexia with something like respect. Something deeper.

The entire room noticed.

Gee raised his glass. "Sounds like a toast to me. To Nalexia—and her vision to transform not just a building, but a community. Cheers!"

Everyone raised a glass.

Except Kimmy.

Her refusal was obvious. Awkward. Petty.

And it reflected badly on Seth.

After the toast, Beckett pulled Nalexia into a quiet embrace and kissed her gently on the temple. The night had been a resounding success.

Nalexia had earned a major win—one that would secure her exit from the firm and elevate her name in the industry. And Beckett? He'd quietly sealed several deals of his own through the evening, contracts linked to affiliate companies where he was a silent investor.

Tonight was more than just a meeting.

It was a demonstration of power.
Partnership. And purpose.

A night where love and strategy met at the same table—and won.

Chapter 19

Rihanna's *"Sex With Me"* pulsed from the car speakers—a fitting anthem for how Beckett felt at the end of the night. He couldn't wait to make love to Nalexia, to remind her how deeply desired she was.

But something was off.

Nalexia sat silently, her gaze fixed out the window. Her body was close, but her mind was somewhere far from him.

Beckett noticed the shift instantly.

She had never been this quiet. Not with him.

He turned the music down and pulled into the lot of a small country store. No hesitation. He reached across the console and took her hand.

"Sweet Bread," he said gently, his voice soft like velvet against skin. "Tell me what's on your mind. What are you thinking about?"

He held his breath. One part of him—the part hardened by past relationships—braced for disappointment. But another part, the deeper one, reminded him that love needed patience.

Nalexia turned off the music completely. Her voice was quiet, almost timid. That alone unsettled Beckett. Nalexia was never timid.

She began to speak—at first carefully, then with growing clarity as the words poured out.

"With everything going on… the firm threatening my contract, my tenants wondering what happens next, and you being so wrapped up in your own world—I've just felt… overlooked."

Her throat tightened as she fought back tears. "Do you know how long I've waited for a love like ours?"

Beckett blinked, stunned.

He had thought the night's victory would leave her on cloud nine. Instead, it magnified the spaces where she still felt unseen.

Nalexia took a breath. "Tonight, we were unstoppable. You fixed every detail I worried about—even the things I only *hinted* at. You called in your affiliates… gave me the leverage I needed. Gee would've been crazy to say no."

She turned to face him fully, her hand caressing his cheek. "Beckett… I love you. You're one hell of a man."

Her voice trembled—but it was full of admiration, not fear. And that single moment cracked something open inside him.

Beckett had craved her physically before. But now? Now the yearning ran deeper than skin. She had seen him—not just for what he could do, but for who he *was*.

He kissed her hand gently and took a slow breath before shifting the car into gear.

"I have a surprise for you," he said.

Nalexia looked at him, confused as he bypassed the exit that would take them back to her apartment.

Instead, he took the BWI Airport exit.

She didn't ask questions.

Within the hour, they were boarding a private flight to the island of Saba.

Beckett had been planning the trip for weeks—a post-deal getaway for celebration. But when Kimmy showed up at the meeting with Seth, he knew *tonight* was the moment. Nalexia needed space. She needed celebration. She needed joy.

When they landed, the crisp salt air and rolling waves were a balm to the soul. The island was breathtaking.

Beckett led her to *The Piano House*, a luxury cottage overlooking the sea—an estate he'd been eyeing for a future smart-home project. Kolani and Torick had insisted the location was a must-see.

Nalexia thought it was just the two of them—until she heard laughter inside the house.

Mitchell and Saleen.

Kolani and Torick.

And El.

They were already there.

The moment Nalexia stepped into the home, her guilt about not being home with her son started to creep in. But then the breeze hit her skin, the scent of citrus and ocean wrapping her in release. *The kids are safe,* she reminded herself. *This is just a long weekend.*

She made a mental note to plan something special with her son when she got back.

The house was stunning. A private chef—booked by Beckett—had laid out a vibrant charcuterie spread on the island countertop. The pool sparkled just outside the window, cascading into a seamless view of the ocean.

From the kitchen, a chorus of female voices echoed. Nalexia followed the sound.

El was the first to see her. "You did it!" she squealed, running into Nalexia's arms.

Next was Saleen. Her tone was calm as always, but the hug was sincere. "Congratulations. Mitchell told me the meeting went even better than expected."

Saleen quickly excused herself and retreated to her room before Kolani entered.

"What is *up* with her?" Kolani muttered, watching Saleen's exit. "How do you have an attitude when your man brings you on a work trip… to a literal paradise?"

Then she turned to Nalexia and squealed, “You did it!”

The women laughed and toasted with cocktails delivered by the chef. Soon Beckett, Mitchell, and Torick joined them. They gathered in a circle, glasses raised.

Beckett’s voice anchored the moment.

“Honey, everything you’ve worked for, everything you’ve dreamed of… you made it happen. Despite setbacks. Despite pressure. You never folded. You’re brilliant. And I’m proud of you.”

“Cheers,” the group echoed, clicking glasses.

Dinner was served on the patio by the pool. The air was warm, the music soft, the laughter rich. Kolani and Torick slipped off for a swim while El and Nalexia wandered down to the beach.

They walked in silence at first, letting the stars and waves speak.

Then El asked something unexpected.

“Does he look the same?”

Nalexia paused, then sat in the sand, close enough for her feet to meet the tide.

"Yeah. He looks the same," she said slowly. "But his attractiveness was a non-factor."

El sat beside her. "What was it like… leading a meeting like that? Big-time investors and all?"

Nalexia smiled, her eyes reflecting the moonlight. "You wanna know the best part?"

"Of course."

"It was realizing that *every single setback* I've had—every delay, every door slammed shut—was preparing me for *that* moment."

El leaned her head against Nalexia's shoulder, quiet with understanding.

They both remembered the dreams they once whispered over cheap wine and takeout—how they'd promised to build something bigger than fear.

And here they were.

Nalexia, standing tall.

Beckett, standing beside her.

And for the first time in a long time, *everything* was starting to feel like home.

Chapter 20

Mitchell sat at the kitchen island, his laptop open, fingers flying across the keys. He was deep in the backend analytics of his latest invention—*Curatestyle*, a smart clothing app that recommended outfits based on users' body shape, size, purchase history, and personal style. For this trip, Beckett had asked everyone to use it to shop for vacation attire as a real-time test.

Mitchell had been monitoring interaction patterns all morning, eager to see how users responded to themes like *tropical luxe* or *casual coastal*. The feedback looked promising.

But not everyone was impressed.

"Do you really have to work on that now?" Saleen's voice rang out, sharp with irritation.

Mitchell didn't look up.

Saleen shifted her weight and crossed her arms. "We are literally in paradise, and you're sitting here glued to a computer screen like we're back in the office."

Before he could answer, she turned and walked out to the pool.

Classic.

Walking away had become her go-to response. No resolution, no real conversation—just distance.

They'd had the same fight every week lately: she wanted presence, he wanted progress. He had hoped this trip would be a reset, a chance for her to see the vision behind his hustle. Instead, she saw the keyboard, not the kingdom he was trying to build for them.

Mitchell sighed and returned to the screen.

A few minutes passed before the sound of the side door opening broke the silence. Elle stepped inside, barefoot, with her hair still damp from the beach. Her face was thoughtful, distant.

Mitchell looked up. "Was the water cold?"

Elle blinked, startled from her thoughts. "I'm sorry—what?"

"I asked if the water was cold," Mitchell repeated, smiling gently.

“Oh.” She offered a small smile. “Not too bad. I just needed to clear my head.”

Mitchell watched her closely. Something about her seemed… off. “You alright?”

Most people would have defaulted to *I’m fine*. Not Elle.

She exhaled and dropped her gaze.

“Actually, no. I’m not okay. I should be overjoyed—my dear friend just reached a major goal and crushed every obstacle in her way. But all I can think about is everything I haven’t done. Everything I *wanted* to do but didn’t.”

She pointed to the chair across from him. “Mind if I sit?”

“Of course,” Mitchell said, surprised by her honesty. He didn’t know Elle well. They’d exchanged polite conversation in the past, but never like this.

Elle opened the fridge, pulled out the leftover charcuterie board the chef had prepared, and set it between them. She passed him a plate, then began stacking crackers with soft cheese, prosciutto, and slivers of dried fruit. Her movements were careful, rhythmic. Like the act of preparing food gave her something to control.

Mitchell appreciated the gesture.

“What are you working on?” she asked between bites.

“My app,” he replied, rotating the laptop screen toward her. “Just checking the data.”

Elle leaned in, chewing thoughtfully. “Oh wow… Congrats. It looks like the app did really well.”

Her comment caught him off guard.

“You know how to read this kind of data?” he asked, genuinely curious.

She wiped her fingers on a napkin. “I do. I process raw numbers and make them digestible. Data analysis is kind of my thing. I used to design presentations for city planning meetings and boardroom proposals.”

Mitchell raised his eyebrows. “Really? You’d be shocked how many inventors I work with who can’t make sense of their own numbers.”

Elle smiled. "That's what makes me useful—I translate dreams into strategy."

Mitchell sat back, impressed. There was something magnetic about her intelligence—not flashy, just solid. Grounded. Easy to miss if you weren't paying attention. But he was paying attention now.

Before the moment could stretch any further, a knock came at the kitchen door. One of the chef's assistants entered with a small package.

Mitchell stood to accept it. "Thanks."

Another knock followed. A security guard entered next, holding a large box. "This one's for Nalexia."

Mitchell used it as an excuse to disengage—he saw Saleen walking back inside from the pool, her face unreadable.

"I'll take that to her," Mitchell told the guard, grabbing the box. Then he turned to Elle, offering a nod. "Thanks for the company."

Elle gave a soft smile. "Anytime."

Mitchell walked off quickly, box in hand, but his mind lingered behind—on the honesty in Elle's voice, the sharpness in her mind, and the feeling of being seen.

It was the most connection he'd felt in days.

And it didn't come from his wife.

Chapter 21

Nalexia finished her shower and dabbed on her signature fragrance. A black crochet nightie clung to her curves, its spaghetti straps resting delicately on her shoulders. She lay across the bed, her legs bare and glistening with oil, waiting.

Beckett walked in and paused at the door. His smile widened when he saw her. She looked like a vision—relaxed, confident, sensual. He closed the door behind him slowly, his eyes never leaving her.

Nalexia lifted her phone and set a ten-minute timer. "Sit," she said, pointing to the chair she'd moved to the foot of the bed. "And don't touch me until the timer goes off."

Beckett obeyed, intrigued.

She pressed play on her playlist, and a sultry beat filled the room. Nalexia climbed onto the bed. Her body moved with deliberate rhythm, dancing, teasing—crawling closer, then pulling away. She never broke eye contact. Her every movement told him exactly how deeply she desired him… but on her terms.

Beckett sat motionless, captivated. His hunger for her had been ignited the second he entered the room, but this—*this*—was something else. She was art and control. Fire and grace.

The timer ticked.

Beckett shifted in his seat, desire thick in his throat.

Nalexia knelt on the bed, still teasing, still owning every second. When the timer went off, the sound pierced the air like a starting gun.

Beckett stood.

In one fluid motion, she was in his lap, her lips pressing against his, her body molded to his like a second skin. The chair scraped back as he stood with her in his arms, kissing her with gratitude and reverence. Their love was more than physical—it was power and safety, trust and release.

They moved to the bed and made love slowly at first, then passionately, both of them lost in the sanctuary they'd created together. After two blissful sessions, Nalexia drifted off mid-sentence, wrapped in Beckett's arms.

Beckett pulled her close, pressing a kiss to her temple, then allowed sleep to claim him too.

Elsewhere in the house, their connection seemed to ripple outward.

Torick and Kolani's laughter echoed behind closed doors, mixing with flirtatious giggles. The chef and one of the staff members were caught in a soft embrace near the pantry, whispering. Passion stirred something in the air.

But not everyone felt it.

Mitchell was back in front of his screen, refining features on his app, trying to ignore the hollow tension between him and Saleen. She lay on the bed beside him, scrolling aimlessly, pretending to be asleep every time he looked over. The silence between them was thick.

Elle lay awake in her room, for the first time aware of her solitude. Talking to Mitchell earlier had awakened something—curiosity, maybe. Or longing. Either way, she missed having someone to talk to, someone who *saw* her.

The next morning, sunlight streamed through the villa's wide windows. Beckett and Torick requested breakfast by the pool, and the chef delivered beautifully. As the house guests stirred, a new face arrived—a modestly dressed man with a warm smile.

"Good morning!" he greeted. "Hope you all are enjoying my little piece of paradise."

Inside, Beckett and Torick spoke with him privately. Elle, seated near the pool, angled her chair to observe the exchange through the glass.

Mitchell appeared, his tablet in hand.

"Who are they meeting with?" Elle asked casually.

"Probably the guy selling the property," Mitchell replied.

"Oh. That makes sense." She smiled. "So... how did you sleep?"

"Fine." His answer was short, eyes still on the screen.

Elle thought about teasing him about the previous night's soundtrack of moans and laughter—but Saleen's arrival from the beach stopped her.

"Good morning," Elle offered politely.

Saleen's reply was cool. "Morning."

The tension made Elle hesitate. She began to gather her plate, preparing to leave.

Mitchell finally looked up. "You're straight. Eat your food."

Saleen made a plate for herself but sat off to the side, far from Mitchell, as if they were strangers. Elle felt a pang—sympathy or sadness, she wasn't sure.

Then Nalexia stepped onto the patio like she'd floated out of a dream. Her cover-up billowed behind her, her shades framed a radiant smile. Someone handed her a peach bellini.

"Well," Nalexia announced, holding her glass high, "it's official. We are now in the vacation home business."

Mitchell smiled. Of course Beckett bought the house. If Nalexia loved it, he'd find a way to turn it into both a retreat and a revenue stream.

Beckett and Torick joined the group. Everyone raised their glasses.

"To living our dreams!" Beckett toasted.

Glasses clinked, joy washed over the group like ocean waves.

As breakfast continued, Beckett addressed the table. "You're all welcome to stay until Tuesday. Nalexia and I are heading back home today to relieve Doc and see the kids. But we'd love for you to enjoy the rest of the weekend. And post lots of photos and videos."

That last line sparked something in Saleen. She perked up immediately, pulled out her phone, and went live while walking toward the beach.

Still sitting across from Mitchell, Elle smirked. "So *that's* all it takes to lift her mood?"

Mitchell looked embarrassed. "Enjoy your food," he mumbled. "I need to check on something before Beckett and Nalexia leave."

He left with his tablet, and Elle watched him go. When Saleen later went live again and mentioned her boyfriend "had business to attend to," Elle realized he hadn't come back to say goodbye.

It stung more than she expected.

Chapter 22

As soon as the plane landed, Beckett was in motion. He had a list for Tyger, a checklist for Mitchell, and a timeline in his head that had no room for delay. The new vacation home needed to be uploaded to every short-term rental platform—Airbnb, Vrbo, and the influencer-only agency Beckett had quietly invested in.

Mitchell trailed behind, juggling final tasks on his tablet when he suddenly realized, "I forgot to schedule a car for you." He touched Nalexia's shoulder as she gathered her things to exit the plane.

She smiled. "It's really okay. Honey can drop me off."

Mitchell nodded, but worry pinched at his chest. Beckett was on a tight schedule—he had a meeting with Lancaster. And Mitchell wasn't sure how much Nalexia knew about the kind of man Lancaster really was. Unscrupulous didn't begin to cover it.

As Beckett and Nalexia pulled away, Mitchell stayed behind to wrap up with the pilot, waving them off with a weighted sense of unease.

Back home, Tyger stood leaning against his slick, low-slung Toyota Supra like a scene from a street racing film. Beckett barely glanced at the car. Flash never impressed him, but Tyger appreciated anything with precision—cars, code, or craftsmanship.

Beckett was underdressed for a business meeting—white tee, blue jeans, Air Max sneakers. Tyger was no better. It was intentional.

As they helped Nalexia inside, she glanced between them. "I thought you two had a meeting?"

Beckett gave her a brief kiss and a reassuring smile. "We do. I'll explain later."

They left quickly.

In the car, conversation flowed casually.

"How'd everything go?" Tyger asked, merging onto the main road.

Beckett's voice was soft with satisfaction. "The house was paradise. A real gem."

"Like our first trip out the country?" Tyger grinned, glancing at him.

Beckett returned the smile. "Exactly. Peaceful. Exciting. It felt like purpose."

Traffic parted for them like fate itself. As they neared the exit, Beckett's phone buzzed—again. Doc had called four times.

Doc was pacing the cracked pavement of an old industrial lot, jaw tight. He wanted all three of them to arrive together, unified. But now, Beckett and Tyger were late.

When Tyger finally screeched into the lot, Doc stormed toward them.

"What the hell are y'all wearing?"

Beckett smirked. "Me in a backwards fitted and tee don't make me a thug, Doc. Re-lax."

Doc wanted to snap back but caught himself as the massive warehouse doors opened. Lancaster stood inside, arms crossed, smug and waiting.

The hollow building amplified the buzz of the cooling fan. Grease-stained cement, metal debris, and the smell of stale oil filled the air.

Lancaster checked his watch. “Hickory Dickory Doc. I thought maybe you finally grew a backbone and skipped out.”

Doc said nothing while he adjusted his clothes. There was a lot of unspoken tension.

“Let’s get this meeting underway,” Lancaster snapped.

Doc made formal introductions, but Lancaster cut him off.

“I’m not interested in meeting these little... thugs of yours. The building’s yours—under one condition: no one knows I sold it. It needs to look like a gift.”

Beckett didn’t blink. “Deal.”

A suited man stepped from the shadows with a folder of documents. Lancaster had already drawn up paperwork declaring Beckett and Tyger as distant relatives. It would appear he gifted them the warehouse out of family obligation.

Beckett glanced at Doc, then signed—purely out of loyalty and respect for Doc. What Beckett didn’t know was that Doc and Lancaster had history. Dirty, twisted history.

Doc had been robbed of his brilliance for decades, with Lancaster always walking away richer. This meeting wasn't just business for Doc—it was deeply personal.

Lancaster handed over the keys and an envelope of legal documents. Then Beckett passed him a black envelope—$250,000 in clean bills. More than it was worth. But that was the point. Beckett wanted Lancaster to feel in control.

What Lancaster didn't know was that Beckett had already launched a rumor on social media claiming the "Lancaster Empire" was being passed down to the next generation. The internet was buzzing. Lancaster's client base would be confused, even suspicious, and that was exactly the disruption Beckett wanted.

The old man smirked, thinking he'd duped a couple of street guys. "Gift" sales weren't taxable income, and he assumed they wouldn't know how to claim the building as a business expense.

But he underestimated them.

Outside, the rumble of a flatbed echoed into the parking lot. Beckett's eyes widened as the massive machinery rounded the corner.

"Tyger, you think this thing's gonna fit?"

Tyger tilted his head. "We'll find out."

Doc walked out just as another surprise pulled up—a repurposed school bus filled with workers in matching uniforms.

"How many square feet is this again?" Doc asked, eyebrows raised.

Beckett laughed. "Enough."

A short guy in a 90s-style windbreaker hopped off the flatbed. "Hey, I'm supposed to meet Mr. Tanger?"

Beckett chuckled. "You mean Tyger?"

Tyger, unamused, corrected him. "Yeah, that's me."

Beckett leaned over. "Where'd you get this thing again?"

Tyger shrugged. "Chick I know found a shut-down plant. Got it for a steal."

Soon, another bus arrived. Over a hundred workers filed out, instantly disassembling the massive machine with surgical precision.

A lead worker approached Tyger. "We need four hours," he said in a thick accent.

Doc's mouth hung open. "You mean to tell me... this'll be built in four hours?"

Tyger nodded. "Take your time," he offered, but the man held up four fingers again with confidence.

Within minutes, the warehouse was alive with the hum of labor, the clang of tools, and the silent choreography of men with a mission.

Beckett stepped over to the driver of the flatbed.

"This all you do?"

The man smiled. "My mom came from Mie, Japan. School visa. Met my dad. They passed when I was ten. I went back to find my roots. Found family. Found purpose. We just want work. Most of us got people overseas. This pays the bills."

Beckett nodded, intrigued. The man texted Beckett his info. Another seed planted for future endeavors.

By the end of the day, the warehouse was transformed. Ready.

So was Beckett.

This wasn't just a warehouse—it was the beginning of an empire.

Chapter 23

Two months later, Beckett stood in the heart of the warehouse—a far cry from the dilapidated building Lancaster had "gifted" him and Tyger. The space had transformed into a powerhouse of innovation and profit, a pillar of the empire they were building. Beckett's chest swelled with quiet pride as he thought about the inventors whose dreams he'd helped bring to life, the breakthroughs he'd enabled—opportunities they never could have seized alone.

Every step of the company's growth had been carefully planned by Beckett and Tyger. The next big move was a complete revamp of the building's infrastructure.

It was Saturday night, but that didn't slow them down. Virtually, Beckett and Tyger hosted Innovation Technologies' first 2 a.m. strategy meeting. Doc glanced at his watch—2:00 a.m. exactly—before bidding his goodbyes. The warehouse was already preparing its third distribution order, and Beckett dove back into work in his home office. Tyger was deeply involved, coordinating onsite with Mitchell, who managed warehouse operations to keep everything running smoothly.

Meanwhile, Beckett's phone buzzed repeatedly. Kimmy was calling. He ignored it, then Tyger's phone lit up as well. Tyger, tangled in a personal crisis, left his phone in the car to avoid answering. Neither noticed the persistent calls.

The next morning, Beckett stood before the cement vault he and Tyger had engineered—a masterpiece of security. Built on Tyger's insights about typical break-in tactics, combined with their sharpest inventor's expertise, the vault was nearly impenetrable.

Seven inches of reinforced cement encased it. The lock triggered only by a precise combination of temperature, facial recognition, and vocal tone. No passwords—only the phrase, *"a means to attain."*

Beckett spoke the phrase aloud, his body scanned, and the vault unlocked. Inside were stacks of cash, keys, and a black envelope marked simply: *Kimmy*.

He closed the vault, rolled the secret wine rack wall back into place, then climbed the five steps separating the cellar from the rest of the house. Passing the kitchen counter, he failed to notice several missed calls blinking on his phone.

Inside his home office, Tyger and the lawyer waited. Beckett closed the door and motioned for Tyger to share everything they'd uncovered on Kimmy.

He handed the black envelope to the lawyer—a tall, bald man with an air of authority who meticulously reviewed the documents. Time seemed to pause as the lawyer digested the evidence.

"Give me a few days," the lawyer finally said. "I'll get back to you."

Everything pointed to Kimmy—the source of their troubles—painstakingly documented in the files.

Beckett slid a neatly folded stack of hundred-dollar bills across the table.

From the other side of the door, the laughter of children and Miss Jeannie's voice filtered in—she'd returned to care for the kids. Beckett told Tyger and the lawyer the meeting had to end. The family needed him now.

The lawyer gathered his things, and Tyger walked him to the foyer.

“How’s everything?” Tyger asked quietly.

“Nalexia’s frustrated. She’d just learned Kimmy had been stalking her for months,” Beckett admitted. “This isn’t going to blow over quickly.” Nalexia slipped out to the office, a moment to get lost in her work.

Hours later, Tyger pulled Becektt into a brotherly hug, then stepped outside.

Inside, the children were lost in video games, tablets, and phones. Beckett sank into the couch, surrounded by their noise and innocence. Miss Jeannie explained she’d be back in the morning to take the kids to swimming lessons and the library.

Beckett thought it odd Nalexia had delegated such tasks, but with Kimmy’s harassment intensifying, communication between them had suffered.

After Miss Jeannie left, Beckett locked the door and glanced at the clock. Hours past Nalexia’s usual arrival time. He reached for his phone—but it was still in the kitchen from the night before.

His curiosity turned to concern when he noticed a missed call from an unknown number and a text from Nalexia sent three hours earlier: *"On my way."*

Beckett called her back—once, twice, then again. No answer.

Nalexia drove north on Route 495, heading toward the Woodrow Wilson Bridge. Rain and fog blurred her vision. Her phone, acting erratically, had been missing calls all day—she suspected Kimmy's handiwork again.

Suddenly, a white SUV slammed into the rear of her car, propelling her vehicle into a terrifying spin.

Four lanes of traffic rushed by as Nalexia gripped the wheel, praying for control.

With instinctive calm, she eased off the gas and lightly tapped the brakes, managing to slow the spin just before hitting the Jersey wall.

The chaos settled. She still gripped the steering wheel tightly—then, unexpectedly, everything went black.

Back at the condo, Beckett's worry deepened. He told himself Nalexia might just need a mental break. But as Kimmy's meddling spiraled, Beckett's anger simmered beneath the surface.

His oldest son, Bradley, broke the silence: "When is Nalexia coming home?"

The question struck Beckett hard. The kids were expecting her. Nalexia wouldn't leave them worried—not like this.

He dialed her number a fifth time.

The call rang three times—then a man answered, voice heavy and cold.

Beckett's mind went blank. The tone of the stranger on the other end shattered his calm.

Bradley noticed the shift in his father's voice.

Quickly, he gathered his siblings and ushered them into the playroom.

Once the kids were settled, Bradley sat in the hallway, earbuds in, searching for answers. Traffic accident reports. A car spinning out on a busy highway. No name released, but pictures showed a wrecked white car—its hood crumpled like paper.

Then, unmistakably, among the wreckage lay a broken coffee mug—one they had all picked out last Mother's Day.

Bradley's heart sank.

He stood, determined, ready to confront his father: Why wasn't Mom home yet?

Beckett's grip tightened around his phone. His voice was steady but fierce as he demanded answers from the stranger on the other end.

The pieces that have fallen into place were now falling apart. And Beckett knew—this was only the beginning.

Chapter 24

Elle’s fingers trembled as she tried calling Beckett again. “I need him to pick up,” she muttered aloud, as if saying it would make it happen. But his phone kept ringing busy.

She gripped the steering wheel of her pale blue Mini Cooper, rain blurring the windshield even with the wipers on full blast. The highway scene before her was a nightmare she could barely believe. She was driving just two cars behind Nalexia, whose vehicle was now part of a chaotic accident.

Police had pulled over both cars, and other drivers were being directed around the wreck. Elle spotted a white SUV with a partially obscured license plate that had cut her off moments before. She tried snapping a picture, but the photo came out blurred.

Elle replayed the sequence over and over in her head. The SUV had darted recklessly through traffic, as if on a mission. The rain had intensified, and visibility was almost zero. The wipers' swish was muted against the storm’s roar.

Then, the horrific moment: she saw one of Nalexia’s shoes lying perfectly on the highway shoulder. She wasn't sure if it had fallen after the car stopped or during the emergency extraction. A faint smell of fried chicken lingered—an odd reminder of a nearby food spot they both liked.

Elle was the only car behind the SUV, and she watched it all unfold in slow motion. The image was seared into her mind.

She glanced up just as the officer approached, waiting patiently.

"It was intentional," Elle blurted, voice shaking.

"Speak up, ma'am?" the officer prompted.

Elle took a deep breath and repeated herself: the accident was no accident. She recounted how the SUV cut her off, then slammed into Nalexia's car, sending it spinning.

She explained that she hadn't realized the driver was someone she knew until she heard the Bluetooth phone ringing in Nalexia's car before the ambulance arrived. "I called her to see if she was ahead of the crash," Elle said. "Then I saw the call come through—'Incoming call for Elle.' That's when I knew the white car belonged to my best friend."

The officer took her statement carefully but didn't confirm Nalexia's condition. The driver who caused the accident had fled on foot into the pouring rain, vanishing into the mist. Tracking him was nearly impossible.

Several other witnesses corroborated Elle's account.

Elle asked the tow driver if she could retrieve personal items from Nalexia's car. He refused but gave her the shop's address where the vehicle was being taken.

She tried Beckett's phone again. Now the line was busy. She hoped he was at least being informed about the accident and that's why he couldn't take her call. Worried he might be stuck on a work call, she dialed his office. The receptionist transferred her to Mitchell.

"Elle, it's been a minute since the island," Mitchell said, recognizing her voice from his social media posts. "Nice to see your number flash across my screen."

Elle's voice cracked. "Mitchell, I'm sorry to bother you, but I need to talk to Beckett."

Mitchell sensed the urgency immediately. "Are you okay?" he asked gently.

Tears spilled down Elle's cheeks as she recounted everything.

Mitchell was on a conference call with two inventors but paused it, immediately calling Beckett and adding Elle on a three-way.

Beckett answered, his voice tight with worry. "I've been trying to reach Nalexia... I needed to keep my phone clear."

Mitchell urged Beckett to stay calm. Elle's sobs echoed through the line.

"Tell me what's going on," Beckett demanded, struggling to maintain control.

Before Mitchell could answer, the doorbell rang.

"Hold on—someone's at the door," Beckett said, his mind racing.

When he opened it, a police officer in uniform and a man in a suit stood there.

Beckett's heart dropped.

Words like *Nalexia*, *intensive care*, *accident*, and *missing driver* reached his ears in fragmented waves.

“The next 48 hours will be touch and go,” they told him.

His thoughts scattered—his children, Nalexia’s grandmother, her clients. Overwhelmed, he stepped away from the door.

The officers looked on, unsure.

Beckett grabbed his phone and shouted, “Mitch!”

Mitchell, sensing the weight of the moment, answered calmly, “Okay, boss.”

Beckett hung up and immediately called Doc. Doc arrived swiftly to stay with the children.

Bradley watched his father’s tense expression. He knew something was wrong but decided to wait until Beckett was ready to talk.

Beckett’s phone rang again.

Kimmy.

He slipped it into his pocket without answering.

Her voicemail was chilling.

Tears choked her voice:

"Beckett, I wish you'd talk to me. I really messed up this time. They were only supposed to scare her... but the rain made it hard to stop. They were only supposed to tap the bumper. Yes, I wanted her to go away, but I didn't mean... for this to happen."

Her voice faltered, heavy with guilt.

"I'm sorry. I'm really sorry. I know you love her..."

Her sobs filled the silence.

"You'll never want me now."

And then the call ended.

The fight is far from over.
To be continued…

www.ingramcontent.com/pod-product-compliance
Lightning Source LLC
LaVergne TN
LVHW090518110826
845146LV00003B/900

* 9 7 9 8 9 9 5 3 6 5 1 0 5 *